LET VENGEANCE BE MINE
A DARK MAFIA BREEDING ROMANCE

LILAH RAINE

Let Vengeance Be Mine
Copyright © 2023 by Lilah Raine
All rights reserved.
First Edition.

No part of this book may be reproduced or transmitted in any form or by any means, electronic or mechanical including photocopying, recording, or by any information storage and retrieval system without written permission of the author, except for the use of brief quotations in a book review.

This is a work of fiction. Names, characters, businesses, places, events and incidents are either the product of the author's imagination or used in a fictitious manner. Any resemblance to actual persons, living or dead, actual events, or locales is entirely coincidental. The use of any real company and/or product names is for literary effect only. All other trademarks and copyrights are the property of their respective owners.

A DARK BREEDING ROMANCE

BY LILAH RAINE

AUTHOR NOTE

Warning
Let Vengeance Be Mine is a work of fiction and contains adult content. Due to the nature of the series you should expect to come across various subject matter that some readers may find disturbing, and it is intended for readers 18+

Please contact the author if you have any questions.

authorlilahraine@gmail.com

PROLOGUE

MATTEO

"Thank you for coming with me today." Thalia smiles warmly as we step out of the private hospital, and walk toward the car I had sent to pick her up this morning. "Here, you can keep this one." She hands me one of the black and white photographs the sonographer printed out for us, and when I look down at the grainy image in my hand, I can't help smiling at it.

A Romano heir, a chance for me to do things so differently.

This was not the way I planned on becoming a father, but fate had other plans, and who the fuck am I to argue with fate?

"I'll have my driver take you home." I look into the pretty, hazel eyes of the woman, who will bring my child into the world, and wonder if I'll ever be able to love her. Thalia's attractive and kind, she knows how to satisfy a man, which is exactly what got us into this situation. But will it be enough?

It will have to be.

I wasn't raised among love, my mother never really paid me much attention as a child. I was brought up by housemaids and nannies, most of who my father would end up fucking and my mother would then fire. For that reason, I always planned to commit myself to one woman. I guess it all just happened a lot faster than I expected.

"Are we still having dinner on Friday night?" Thalia looks up at me with a hopeful smile. It's not often we spend time with just the two of us. We've only ever hooked up after parties, but now all that is going to change. I will give our child stability. If we have a son I will teach him how to respect, and if we have a daughter she will know how to be respected.

"Of course. I shall have Claude pick you up at seven," I assure her.

"And it will be just the two of us?" she checks.

"Three," I remind her, sliding my hand over her flat stomach, unable to keep the smile off my face.

"How could I forget?" She giggles before reaching up on her toes to place an awkward kiss on my cheek.

"*We'll* see you Friday then," she tells me.

I watch her move toward the car she came in, and when one of my new drivers goes to open the door for her, a thought comes to mind when I look down at the picture in my hand.

"You should take my car, you have a longer journey and it's far more comfortable."

I move over to my own car and open the back passenger door, for her, myself. Franco has been my driver since I was twelve years old, I trust him with my life, and now he will be trusted with the life of my child.

"Honestly, Matteo, there's no nee–"

"I insist. Franco, get Miss Cattaneo home, safely. Remember, you have precious cargo on board," I order my driver, who nods at me efficiently as he gets behind the wheel. Once she's inside, and I've closed the door for her, she waves as he pulls into the heavy city traffic.

. . .

I can tell by my best friend's face that he disagrees with what I'm doing, he's been on edge all morning and he looks even more worried now that he can see the evidence in my hands.

"Speak your mind," I call out to him.

"I already have...Did you ask her to move into the house, yet?" Demitri moves to stand beside me as we watch them drive away.

"Not yet. I don't want to push her, getting her to keep the child was enough for now. I'll gradually work towards the next step."

"Do you ever wonder if, maybe, she did it on purpose?" His next question has me moving fast, gripping my best friend by his throat and pressing him into the side of the car.

"Why would she do that? Her father is one of the richest men I know. She could have any man she wants. What reason would she have to tie herself to me?" My eyes narrow on him as I wait for his answer.

"Some women are attracted to power, and you, my friend, have a lot of it." "I know where the mistake was made, and it was a lack of control on my part. The outcome is a gift, not a burden." Slowly I release him, keeping the snarl on my lips. A loud bang suddenly echoes through the tall buildings that tower around us. Pulling my attention away from Demitri so I can look up the street in the direction that it came from. What I see there is pure chaos. Thick, black smoke bellows in the air. People are on the floor crawling to safety, trying to get away from the car that's burst into flames.

A car that belongs to me...

CHAPTER ONE

MATTEO

ONE YEAR LATER

"I really don't think this is a good idea." Demitri struggles to keep up with me as I march down the narrow, underground corridor. "She's Stevan Fucchini's daughter," he points out, as if that isn't the whole reason why the girl, I have in my basement, is here.

I stop when I get to the door and turn around.

"I'm very fucking aware of that." I stare my best friend right in the eye. He always was far too hesitant.

"I'm just asking you to think about this, she doesn't know who's taken her yet, she hasn't seen anybody's face. We could return her and no one would be any wiser."

"Return her?" I scoff a laugh at him.

"The little bitch belongs to me now. He took from me, and now, I take from him," I put it simply. I've spent a long time coming up with this plan. I will not back out now when my vengeance is so close.

"I'm not going stand by and watch you kill an innocent girl, Matteo, that's not what you're about."

I smile because he almost sounds like he's trying to threaten me.

"You think I want to kill her?" I laugh again. Demitri has been my friend for as long as I can remember, I expected him to know me better than that.

"Then what is she here for? Why did you have your men travel across the country to bring her here?"

"Because she will give me what her father denied me. I'm going to fuck the next Romano heir into her womb, and end this feud once and for all." Demitri's eyes widen and when he takes a step back, the look on his face suggests he's judging my sanity.

"Matteo, I think I preferred the plan where you kill her. You can't force her to carry your child. She's practically a fucking princess!"

"There is no royalty in our world, anymore. We are all just men fighting for power. My family has always had a strong bloodline, but I will make it stronger."

"You think this is going to result in an alliance with the Fucchini's? Matteo, the man wants you dead. The bomb that blew up your car, and killed Thalia, was meant for you." His reminder has me balling up my fists.

"I don't want an alliance. I want justice."

"Matteo." Demitri grabs my hand when I take the handle of the door. "You've always been a ruthless bastard when it came to getting what you want, but you've always respected women. This isn't you."

"This is me, now." I shove him away.

"This is going to cause a war."

"I'm counting on it." I smile back at him over my shoulder before opening the door. Not even his final attempt to talk me out of this will cause me to hesitate.

Though, seeing her in the flesh for the first time, has me standing still. Fucchini's daughter has been stripped to her underwear, on my orders. She stands blindfolded, with her mouth gagged, and her neck chained to my basement wall by a metal collar. I have to confess it's a beautiful sight to behold.

I already knew the girl was pretty, from the pictures I have seen, but what I'm seeing displayed in front of me now, is quite exquisite.

Her legs are long and look as if they've been kissed by the sun. Her stomach is flat and toned, but it won't be staying that way for long. I plan for her to be carrying my child as soon as possible. Licking my lips, I raise my eyes over her tits and I admire the way they spill, ever so slightly, over the top of her bra.

I take my time as I approach her, admiring the way she holds her breath to brace herself when she senses me getting close. It makes me wonder if this pretty, little 'princess' has even been touched by a man before.

She hitches her breath, again, when I'm standing in front of her and as my nose slides up her cheek, absorbing her scent, she keeps hold of that breath as her body shivers.

I want to touch her with my lips to see how she tastes, but more than that I want her to feel fear.

Pulling slightly back, I slowly raise the blindfold over her head and watch her eyes adjust to the dim light. They fix straight onto mine and, like a deer in the headlights, she doesn't blink, just stares at the threat and waits for it to strike.

My finger slides over her cheek before I hook it into the fabric that's tied around her mouth and drag it under her chin.

"Speak your name." I grasp her jaw in my hand, forcing her to look up at me.

Her eyes lose all that bewilderment, narrowing at me like she's casting some kind of curse.

"You know my fucking name." When she talks back to me, my fingers automatically squeeze tighter, puckering her thick, juicy lips together.

"I didn't ask you *what* your name was, I told you to fucking *speak it!*"

The girl glares at me maliciously as I release her mouth, sliding my hand down her throat so she can talk.

"Aria." She scowls at me.

"And do you know why you are here, Aria?" I keep my voice low and try to ignore the tingle of thrill I'm feeling in my fingertips.

She shakes her head and I swear I see a tear start to form before she bravely blinks it away.

"You're here because your daddy fucked with the wrong man." My fingers slip lower, brushing between her pert, little tits. I regret having my guard strip her down to her underwear now, that pleasure should have been mine. Taking one of those tits in my palm, I crush it, making a gasp slip from her lips and her eyes close, almost like she finds a little pleasure in my touch.

"You're here because he is unable to protect you," I remind her of the position she's in, in case she's forgotten.

Lowering my touch to her tight, flat stomach, I spread my fingers wide and slip them under the waistline of her white, cotton panties.

"And you're *here* because you are going to give me something very special." My lips touch against her neck, feeling her pulse beat against them, and the scared little whimper she makes into my ear makes my cock hard.

Slowly, my middle finger slides between her pussy lips and she proves she's not the innocent, little being I'm sure her father thinks she is when she dampens it. I do nothing to hide the smirk from my face as I arch my free hand under her chin and grip so tight my fingers shake.

"Don't be scared. I think you're going to enjoy the things I do to you, Aria." Raising my slick finger from between her legs, I trail it around her lips to coat them in her disgrace.

The girl wasn't supposed to take pleasure in what will happen to her but, I have to admit, I like the irony in it. Fucchini's precious, little princess, whose marriage has probably been arranged since before she could walk, begging to be fucked by his enemy. I like the idea so much, I decide to set myself the challenge.

I watch her lips rub together when she tastes herself on them and the way her eyes flutter, as she blushes from it, proves this will be far too easy.

"Good night, Aria." I drag myself away, leaving her chained to the wall like an animal, as I head toward the door.

"Wait, are you just going to leave me here?"

The fear in her voice gets my dick even harder and I pause, turning my head to take one final look at her before I leave.

"For now." I feel the dark grin pull on my lips before I exit and slam the door behind me.

"Matteo." Demitri meets me at the top of the stairs. If he hasn't made it clear enough that he thinks this is a bad idea, the worried look on his face says it all.

"Relax, it went well." I march past him toward my office, leaving the door open for him to follow me. I pour myself something strong and leave the stopper off the decanter, so he can help himself. Then, taking a seat behind my desk, I wait for him to start his lecture.

"So, what now? You can't keep her chained down there until you've knocked her up. That could take months, and what then? She will need medical treatment during the pregnancy.

You haven't thought this through." Demitri shakes his head, getting more and more agitated as he paces.

"You'll give yourself a heart attack"

I light myself a cigarette before taking a file from my drawer and throwing it on the desk in front of me.

"What is this?" He picks it up and starts flicking through the information inside.

"That is Joseph Fabier, he specializes in fertility but also has an impressive history in obstetrics. I want you to bring him to me." I blow a cloud of smoke into the air and rest back in my chair, kicking my feet up on the desk and letting my mind wander back to the little creature I have chained in my basement. I really hope daddy's been keeping her a virgin in preparation for her suitor. The benefits will soon be mine if he has.

"And there's nothing I can say to convince you that this is a bad idea?" Demitri interrupts my train of thought.

"No." I shake my head, keeping a very serious look on my face.

"I'll send Ludo and Enzo to fetch the doctor." Demitri gives up trying to reason with me, tucking the folder under his arm and heading out of my office with a displeased look on his face.

Just like his father was to mine, Demitri is loyal, but he's never been a go-getter.

I pull open my desk drawer and take out the sonogram picture Thalia handed me just before she died. I'll never know if our child was a boy or a girl, or if it had my eyes. Fucchini will pay for that. Whether or not his daughter does too, will be a matter of her opinion.

CHAPTER TWO

ARIA

How did I get here? One minute, I'm enjoying a peaceful stroll on my father's private beach, while all my so-called friends slept off their hangovers. Next, I'm being hauled away by the masked men who brought me here.

I fought like a Fucchini should. I punched, I bit and I scratched like a tiger. But there were five of them. Five strong men who I stood no chance against.

Now, I'm here in a cold, damp room, stripped to my underwear with my neck chained to a wall, and my pulse throbbing wildly. The shiver on my skin isn't from the cold, it wasn't there until I saw *him*. I didn't feel the butterflies in my stomach until he lifted that blindfold and his dark eyes singed into mine.

I'm ashamed of the way I reacted to his touch, humiliated by the amount of men who have seen me in my underwear in the past 24 hours and the only positive I can pull from this situation, is the fact that the man who took me is going to die a very slow, painful death.

Nobody takes Stevan Fucchini's daughter and lives...

The door opens and when my host returns I make a conscious effort not to look him in the eyes, again.

I immediately fail.

The man in front of me is far too handsome to ignore. He's tall and well-built. The black shirt he's wearing fits over his muscles like a glove. And I really shouldn't be focusing on how chiseled his scruff-covered jaw is, as he scratches his tattooed fingers through it and studies me.

"How are you?" His voice is smooth and calm as he positions himself directly in front of me.

I respond by pulling my head back and spitting right into his handsome face. His dark, brown eyes penetrate anger into mine, as he wipes the saliva from the crease of his nose. Then, taking some time to scrutinize the way it looks on his fingers, he shocks me by slipping them between his lips and sucking them clean.

"Mmm," he growls deeply, his forehead creasing as he tastes me. "Looks like we will have to work on your manners. I expected better from a princess." The way he speaks so calmly gets right under my skin and I swear, if my ankles weren't shackled to the ground, I'd raise my knee and smash him in his balls.

"I apologize for the late intrusion." His fingers twist around a strand of my hair as he talks.

"I'm not a very good sleeper." His touch lowers over my body and sets off a desire inside me that shouldn't be there. "I will confess, you are much prettier than I thought you would be. What I'm going to do to you won't be much of a chore to me, at all." My skin shivers when he lazily traces his fingertips along my panty line and causes my pussy to automatically tense. It's all kinds of wrong that I crave to feel him there again, and I have to do all I can not to show it. This won't be forever, it's only a matter of time before my father finds out where I am.

"You are going to die for this," I warn, my father may not have spent much time with me growing up, but the one thing I do remember him teaching me, was never to show fear.

My captor's straight lips hook up into a smile, one that I shouldn't be finding attractive.

"Maybe." He shrugs. "If that is to be the case, I hope you are worth it." Dropping his head, he places a gentle kiss on my forehead and I struggle against my restraints to fight him off.

His cool instantly falters and he shoves my body hard into the wall behind me, bracing himself against the bricks with his palm, while his other hand slowly slides up my thigh and creeps inside my panties.

"All I've thought about, up there, is whether or not you are pure." His whisper isn't soft anymore, it's harsh and vicious.

And, as two of his fingers stroke against my sensitive flesh, I tense my body and try to hold in my reaction.

"You're wet, Aria," he points out, mockingly. "Soaking, fucking, *wet*. Far too *wet* to be a virgin." His lips brush against my cheek as he speaks and I have to bite my lip to stop myself from moaning.

"I think I should investigate this matter...a little *deeper*. What do you think?"

My head shakes back at him.

"Your head says no, but your pussy is telling me something *very* different." He strokes me some more with his fingers and, instead of shaking my head, I fix my eyes on his and wait.

My heart beats rapidly in my chest as the two fingers he's pleasuring me with, edge closer to my entrance and I feel all my muscles clam up.

"You tense like you're afraid." A malicious snigger follows his words, making me want to punch it off his face but, instead, I dig my nails into my palms and wait for what comes next.

"Breathe." He remains calm, inhaling deep with me as he

teasingly circles his finger around my entrance. "Relax." His voice somehow soothes me enough to exhale and, as I do, he slowly slips his finger inside me.

"Mmmm." He makes the same satisfied sound he made when he tasted my saliva off his fingers, and it triggers my body to squeeze around the finger he has seated inside me.

"That's a good girl." His praise fulfills something inside that I didn't realize was missing; and as he slowly pulls out and pushes back in, he gifts me with a sensation that feels both uncomfortable and thrilling, at the same time.

"You're so fucking tight. My cock is going to rip you apart," he threatens, with a hint of laughter in his tone. I *hate* it, even if that threat is what is making me soak his finger. And when he slides another one inside me, stretching me further, the pad of his thumb softens the sting by applying some pressure to my clit.

I can feel something building up inside of me, something that makes the ground feel like it's disappearing and the air around me harder to suck in. His fingers slip in and out of me so much easier because of how wet I'm making them, and when his tongue slides up my throat, and his teeth nip my ear, my stomach threatens to explode.

I whimper like an injured puppy when I feel the pleasure start to brim. Then, suddenly, his fingers pull away, leaving me with a dull, aching throb in the pit of my stomach and making me want to claw the smirk, he makes back at me, off his face.

"It seems I will be your first." He takes his soaked, wet fingers and traces them over the skin on my stomach as if he's marking me.

"You could have just asked." Not once in the hours since I have been taken have I cried, but I feel the threat of tears now.

It's ridiculous and only confirms the power this man could have over me if I let him.

"Where would the fun in that have been?" He shakes his head as he skims those magic fingers over my panties, to tease me some more.

"We will get started tomorrow, I suggest that you are compliant. I think I've proven that I can make this bearable for you. But I'll warn you that I'm not renowned for my tolerance." Turning his back on me, he starts to walk back towards the door.

"Please!" The word tumbles out of my mouth, and I'm so confused, I don't know if I'm begging him to come back or to let me go.

"That's a really good start, Aria." He smiles wickedly before leaving me alone for the second time today.

CHAPTER THREE

MATTEO

I sit at the breakfast table waiting for the door to open and when it does, one of my guards drags Fucchini's feisty daughter into my dining room. She struggles against him and I get a strange satisfaction from the fact she immediately pauses when she sees me. I still haven't permitted her any clothes, just clean, black, lace underwear which I think compliments her golden skin tone. It also makes me decide I don't like the way Ludo's hands look on her.

"Release her," I order, watching as the girl studies the space around her, appearing overwhelmed. I'm not stupid enough to buy it though, The grandeur of my dining hall won't be something Aria is unfamiliar with, her father is a very rich man, she will be used to these kinds of luxuries. What I predict is that she's getting her bearings, and looking for an escape route. One that she won't find. I've got this place locked down like fucking Alcatraz.

"Join me." I gesture my hand to the space that's been laid for her, beside me. I know she will be hungry. The stubborn, little bitch has returned every meal I've had Anita send down for her since she's been here, and given what I have planned for her, that will not do.

She snarls at me like a wolf as she moves closer, and just watching the way her body moves has me wanting to snatch her in my hands and destroy her all over my breakfast table.

But first things first, the girl must eat.

"Please, help yourself." I nod my head toward the food that's spread out on the table, watching her eyes wander hungrily over the pastries and fruit that Anita has prepared. I decide to set an example by reaching forward and picking up an apple for myself.

Aria doesn't react, she just watches me bite into it with that hateful look in her eyes.

"Starving yourself isn't going to do you any good. Your body needs to be in good condition for what I have planned for it," I inform her, keeping my voice casual.

"And what, exactly, do you have planned for it?" She tilts her head, trying desperately to put on a brave face.

It's harder than I expected to answer her question. Up until the moment her eyes locked onto mine downstairs, putting my child inside her was my only intention. Now, I want to put my child inside her while she begs me for it.

That's dangerous. I'm fully aware that I can not become attached to this woman and, yet, it's hard not to form an attachment to something that looks so beautiful.

"How old are you, Aria?" I avoid her question by asking her something I already know.

"I'm nineteen." She looks back at me with a strong will and determination that I can't wait to break.

"And how are you still a virgin?" I take another bite of the apple in my hand and wait for her answer, and all she does is shrug her shoulders.

"Does your father have plans for you to marry?" I continue my questioning.

"You'll have to ask him." She's getting smart with me and instead of angering me, like it should, I can't control the smirk it puts on my face.

"Me and your father aren't exactly on speaking terms," I tell her, tamping down the rage that starts to build in my chest when I think about Stevan Fucchini. Now isn't the time for this girl to be getting a rise out of me. I must be in full control when I'm around her.

"How about you and I make a deal, Aria? I'll be honest with you if you are honest with me. Who has your father promised you to?" I rephrase my question. Her answer is valuable to me, it will give me an insight into what direction Fucchini plans to take his empire.

There's an immediate change to the girl's attitude, her posture changes, her shoulders sag and those pretty eyes fall to the table.

"Dennis Jefferson," she mumbles the name and when I laugh at her words, she looks up at me with a sadness on her face that tells me she's being serious.

"The man must be almost sixty," I say my thoughts out loud and when she nods her head back at me timidly, something that feels a lot like empathy wedges in my throat.

"I'm assuming you aren't happy with this arrangement?" I lean forward in my chair so I can study her more closely. Sorrow looks exquisite on her.

Her eyes almost look like they're pleading with me for help when she slowly shakes her head at me. The beauty in her vulnerability almost has me forgetting that she's my enemy's daughter.

"Now, it's your turn." She pulls in a brave breath,

attempting to regain some of that strength she's trying to show. "What do you intend to do with my body?"

I study her a little longer, sliding my finger over my bottom lip and imagining all the things I have planned. Then, taking the plate that's in front of her, I add some fruit and one of Anita's pancakes to it before placing it back.

"Eat that, and I'll show you." I sit back in my chair and watch with intrigue as she picks up her fork and, with a look of discontent, does exactly as I say.

CHAPTER FOUR

ARIA

This is all one big head-fuck. Whoever this man is, he's not my friend, and yet something inside me feels drawn to him. I shouldn't have told him what I just did, knowledge is power, and the vibes I'm getting from him tells me he has enough of that.

"Take her to the room," he orders the guard, who brought me in here, when I've eventually cleared my plate and, as he steps toward me and roughly takes my arm, my whole body instantly stiffens.

"I don't think *force* is necessary, Tomas." My captor reaches forward and eases him off. "I'm sure Miss Fucchini will be compliant. There are no means of escape for her." He smiles at me through his threat, and when I nod back at him obediently, Tomas lets me go. I won't show all my cards here, but I *will* find a way out of the mess I'm in. For now, I believe my best form of defense is to let this man believe I can be *compliant.*

I wipe my mouth with my napkin and place it back on the table before standing up and following Tomas out the dining room, willingly. When we get to the door, I look back over my shoulder and notice how my captor's head is slightly tilted and checking out my ass. The blush it puts on my cheeks doesn't belong there but I smile at him, regardless. If it's games he wants to play, becoming a competitor is the only way for me to win.

I don't know if I'm more excited, or nervous, as Tomas leads me up the impressive staircase. My toes sink into the soft, red carpet and I admire some of the artwork on the walls before we stop at a door and he pushes it open, gesturing for me to enter. The first thing I notice, which brings with it a whole lot of relief, is a bed. Complete with a mattress, some pillows and a comforter, it's a welcome sight after spending two nights sleeping on a cold, damp floor. The decor of the room matches the elegance of the rest of the house, even if it is practically empty of any furniture.

"Through here." Tomas goes to grab me again, but the stern look I give him seems to remind him of his boss's words. He clears his throat and opens the door on the other side of the room, one that leads into a bathroom.

Inside there is plenty of space, but like the bedroom, everything is minimal. There are bars on the window and not even a mirror on the wall, but I see that the bath has already been drawn, and when Tomas nods his head towards it, I step forward and test the temperature with my fingertips.

"You don't honestly expect me to bathe in front of you, do you?" I laugh at him, trying my best to show confidence. The big brute may look scary but he's just as much of a slave to the man downstairs, as I am.

"No, Miss, but I will be right outside." He winks sarcastically before stepping out and closing the door behind him. As soon as I'm alone, I start searching around for a way out.

I test the bars on the window to confirm they're solid, but even if they weren't it would be far too small for me to climb out of. I check the cupboard under the basin and find it empty, all I have to work with is a towel, a sponge and a bar of soap that smells heavenly.

After assessing all my options, and deciding that there is no way out of here, I slip out of my panties and take off my bra, sinking myself into the hot, foamy water and admitting defeat...for now.

I feel my muscles relax as I breathe in the aromas around me and taking the sponge and soap, I lather up my body.

I take my time, enjoying my freedom away from the basement despite still being confined, and when I'm ready to face reality again, I get out of the tub and wrap the towel, that's neatly folded on the basin, around my body. I'm surprised that when I open the door, to step back into the bedroom, instead of Tomas standing guard, I see *him* sitting in the chair in the corner of the room. His elbows rest on its arms, his fingers cross in the middle, and I feel his stare as his eyes slowly assess me. My pussy responds in a way that has me closing my eyes and swallowing down my shame.

"How was your bath?" His voice sounds soothing as I take a few more steps into the room.

"Good." I cling to the towel I have wrapped around my chest.

"Good," he repeats my word with a hint of sarcasm, nodding his head as he stands up and moves towards me. I hold my breath as he stalks a slow circle around my body. And although his hands don't touch me, I still feel him on my skin, and it doesn't make it crawl the way it should. It makes it tingle with something I fear could be desire.

Once he's standing in front of me again, my eyes automatically look up into his, and the serious look on his handsome face makes me release that breath I've been holding on to, a little too loudly.

"Take off the towel." His words aren't quite whispered, but they come out much softer than I expected. Soft enough to not have me resisting. I'm in no position to argue with him and, wrong as it may be, I like having this man's eyes on my body. I like his attention, and I like the thrill it puts in the pit of my stomach.

He looks down at my naked body but shows no reaction to it. Eventually, his hand reaches out, and his fingers slowly trace over the skin on my neck, past my shoulder and trail the outline of one of my tits. The sensation of them makes a gasp catch in my throat.

"Ask me, again." His fingers spread out over my stomach, steadily lowering toward my pussy.

"Ask what?" I hear the tremble in my voice and realize it isn't coming from fear.

"Ask what I intend to do to your body, Aria," he reminds me of my earlier question, pausing his touch just before he reaches the place where I crave to feel it. I look up at him through my lashes and pull together all my confidence so I can ask him again.

"What will you do to my body?" I whisper the words as I stare into his cold, dark eyes.

"I'm going to break it." His hand cups my pussy while his other wraps tight around my throat, forcing me roughly onto the mattress, and pinning me down with his grip. Despite my shock, I manage to look up at him and put on a smile.

This man wants my fear so badly, he'll use it to get himself off, and I won't give it to him. If he thinks he can break me, let him try. Anything is better than Dennis-fucking-Jefferson.

"I'm gonna fuck that smile right off your face," he warns me, and I shock him further by spreading my legs to make it easy for him. Yeah, I'm nervous, I know it's going to hurt and I'm certain he won't be gentle, but even I know that the tension, he's put inside me, isn't going to be released until he takes me.

He looks down at me and frowns, shaking his head like his plan is falling apart. The confidence, that my plan is already working, helps me tip him over the edge by reaching my hand between my legs and rubbing my finger against the throb he's created.

His brow creases deeper as he snatches at my wrist and swipes it away, then it's my turn to be shocked when he drops to his knees, grips my thighs and buries his head between my legs.

His tongue attacks my sensitive flesh, feasting on me like a starved animal, as his fingers indent my skin.

I lift my hips off the mattress so I can take more of it, and when he pulls back so he can look up at me, he fixes his eyes on mine as he spits sharply at my clit. I watch him use his finger to mix his saliva with the wetness his tongue has created and when he sinks those soaked fingers inside me, any efforts I make not to show weakness, fail me when I moan.

His head lowers back down so he can give me his tongue again, flicking at my clit, hard and fast while his fingers fuck me, almost painfully. Yet, I feel myself clenching tight to them, scared he'll pull away. Something inside me contracts and it makes my toes curl and my hips buck uncontrollably against his mouth. All that tension I've been holding on to releases itself from my body with a force I can't control and as I soak his tongue, his eyes narrow on mine while he watches my undoing.

I press my hand to my head, to try and stop it from spinning, and his body climbs up the bed, forcing it away and pinning it to the mattress. He bites at my lip before filling my mouth with his tongue, forcing me to taste myself off him, as his fingertips bruise my wrist, and his other hand takes my throat again.

"You taste that?" He looks down on me, focusing hard on my swollen lips. "*That's* what I'm gonna take. I'm gonna fuck your tight, innocent, little pussy until it fucking bleeds, and then I'm gonna fuck it some more." His threat makes my core throb as he drags his hand from my throat and rips his belt from its buckle. I watch him force the slacks off his hips, and my eyes widen when his huge, solid cock lands hard and heavy against my stomach. Now, I *know* I'm in some real trouble.

CHAPTER FIVE

MATTEO

I watch her pretty eyes stretch wide, as she looks down between us and sees my cock for the first time. Now, the confident, little bitch looks scared. She may have, somehow, managed to manipulate an orgasm from me before we got started; I was weak to give in to the temptation, but now I'm feeling like I've got the upper hand again. I can still taste her on my lips, and the moan she made as she came all over my tongue makes me fucking determined to hear it, again.

Taking my cock in my hand I guide it through her pussy lips, coating its tip with her pleasure and feeling her sensitive clit still pulse. This will be a challenge, I felt how tight Aria is when she clutched around my fingers and I can't imagine what my cock will do to her. What I do know is that it will be an experience I won't want to forget.

She watches me, as I press myself against her delicate, little opening. I feel the tension in her fingertips as they grip my biceps and she braces herself. She still has that savage look on her face, but it falters when she takes a brave breath and nods her head at me, almost like this is what she needs. Sinking inside her feels like an out-of-body experience. It must be...

because, right now, I don't feel like I'm in the body of the man who wanted to hurt this woman. What I want to do, is fucking worship her. I want to take my time and make sure she feels every hard inch of me stretch her pussy and make it mine. Her body feels so fucking good as it tries to resist me and as I admire the discomfort on her face, it assures me that the man I really am isn't too far away.

When I'm fully seated inside her, I give her body some time to adjust and the pain, she stares back at me with, morphs into something that looks almost grateful. I try really hard to figure her out. Have I been too kind? Given her the wrong message? This girl is not here for fucking pleasure, and yet here I am wanting to make this experience feel good for her. I watch her hands slowly move up to frame my face, and when reality strikes, I react quickly by tossing them away.

I must train her to understand what this is, and that lesson must begin now. Keeping her throat in my hand, I squeeze my fingers tight as I pull out my cock, and slam it back into her again.

Aria's eyes widen in shock and she whimpers, as her freshly-broken pussy clamps around my cock like a vice. It feels fucking good, so good that she's gonna have me coming inside her way sooner than I intended. Her hands wrap around the wrist I'm pinning her with, and when she starts to make those sweet, little noises again, I slide my hand up to cup her chin and force my fingers into her mouth, so I can silence her.

I thrust in and out of her, feeling how she soaks my cock and fingers, at the same time. The tension in her body begins to loosen and I watch her body move to my rhythm as her thighs tremble against my hips and edges me closer.

"I'm going to come so deep inside you, I'll be spilling from you for days," I warn, making her head shake against my hand as she tries to force it from her mouth. I raise my eyes up from watching us connect, and the desperate look in her eyes takes me over the fucking edge.

I growl deep, clutching at her hip as she bites the fingers I have wedged in her mouth and makes muffled sounds that sing to the devil in my soul.

My cock pulses inside her, filling her virgin cunt with my seed and when I slowly remove my fingers from her mouth those words, she was so desperate to get out, don't seem to come. Carefully, I drag my cock out of her, and when I see my blood-streaked cum leak from her freshly-broken hole, I use two of my saliva-soaked fingers to force it back inside her.

"I...I'm not on any birth control," she tells me, shaking her head and looking down at the hand I'm using, to ensure my cum remains inside her.

"I know." I watch more panic take over her face, her head slowly shaking back at me as it dawns on her what's happening here.

"Are you *crazy?*" She stares into my eyes like I'm some kind of psychopath. Maybe I am because as I push my cum-soaked fingers as far into her body as I can get them, to make sure my seed takes its hold inside her, I allow myself the pleasure of her fear.

"You are gonna give me so much more than just your pussy, sweet, little Aria." I bite at her lip and drag it a little before I pull my fingers from inside her and lift myself off the bed. Picking up her towel from the floor, I toss it at her so she can cover herself and head for the door.

"Make sure she doesn't stand up for at least 30 minutes," I instruct Tomas, who's standing guard outside. Then, taking one last look at the stunned, little mess I've left on the bed, I smile to myself and head for my office.

CHAPTER SIX

ARIA

I end up back in the basement and, as I sit and stare at the dark, brick walls, I wonder how the hell I'm going to get out of this mess. When one of the guards brings down dinner, I eat it. Today's events have exhausted me too much to be stubborn. What happened earlier in the bedroom was both incredible and disastrous all at the same time. I'm sore, my legs are still shaking, and the fact he came inside me while knowing that I'm unprotected, proves this man has no morals at all. The guard nods his head at me after I've finished eating then, taking the plate away, he leaves me alone again.

Being confined down here is its own form of torture. I miss conversation, I even miss the people I pretend to be friends with. It's only been a few days but I feel like I've forgotten what sunlight and open space feel like.

I don't know how late it is when the basement door opens, but when I see *him* step through it, I quickly stand up, keeping my back pressed against the wall that my collar is chained to. He carries a glass in his hand and steps close enough that we're almost nose to nose.

"Why did you give yourself to me so willingly?" He tilts his head and studies me as if I intrigue him.

"How did you know I wasn't on birth control?" I hit back, doing my best to remain strong.

"I asked my question first." His deep glare ensures I feel his dominance.

"I figured you were gonna take me anyway. You brought me here against my will, it was inevitable that you would fuck me against it too." I give him half of the truth, there is no way I'm going to admit that my body actually desired him.

"Now, answer mine, how did you know?" I hold my head up confidently.

"I had one of my men look into your medical records." He shrugs as if that's not a big deal.

"You can't do that again." I shake my head, hearing how desperate my voice sounds when it becomes impossible to hide my desperation. I can't let this happen. I'm in a bad enough situation as it is.

The man who has my future in his hands doesn't seem to be listening to me. He's too focused on the glass in his hand that he lazily strokes across my lower stomach. The ice inside it feels cold against my skin, and it causes my nipples to harden beneath the bra I'm wearing.

"Who says I can't?" He slowly moves his gaze back up my body until those dark, brown eyes glare into mine, daring me to say, '*Me.*'

"It's dangerous. I could end up preg—"

"You *will* end up pregnant. I'm going to make sure of it." The lopsided grin he makes is devilishly handsome and almost distracts me from what he just said. "I'm going to be really honest with you, *Aria*." The way he says my name sounds spiteful. "More honest than I should be." My heart beats fast as I await his confession. "You intrigue me in a way I did not expect. You've been on my mind ever since I left you upstairs dripping with my cum." The way he makes those dirty words sound has my sore pussy starting to ache even more. "I wanted to give your pussy some time to recover. But I need a release, and it seems like such a waste if that release isn't inside you." My chest tightens and I have to really reach to take my next breath.

"How sore are you, Princess?" He asks, almost sounding concerned.

"Very," I admit, though a huge part of me regrets it. I don't know if I want him to take pity on me or not. He smiles at me again, as if he finds amusement in my suffering and then taking my wrist with his free hand he forces my palm to feel how solid he is beneath his slacks.

"You feel that? How hard that is? It's all for you. What am I to do with it, Aria?" It almost sounds as if he's giving me the option, and although my body is begging me to tell him to give it to me, my head is screaming for me to tell him to go screw himself.

"Why do you want to get me pregnant?" I massage my palm across his slacks, hoping it will help bring me some answers.

"Why, is not what's important." He finishes the contents in his glass and throws it against the far wall, making the glass shatter and my body jolt. Then resting both his palm against the wall behind me he leans his head closer to mine. "What you *should* be focused on is giving me what I want. And taking *from* me what you need." He unbuckles his belt, letting his cock fall free, and when I look down and see his hand wrapped around it, I watch in fascination as he pumps it through his fist.

"Take off your panties." He breathes heavily, as he fucks his hand, and without any hesitation, or resistance, I slide them off my hips and let them fall to my ankles.

"You caused this." The tip of his cock presses against my stomach, and I feel it leak a little onto my skin. "You will take it, and you will clutch it inside your hot, little cunt, do you understand?" His voice gets more and more aggressive as he works his fist harder. There's an uncontrollable throb between my legs now, one that has me nodding my head back at him like I'm the puppet and he's the master.

"Good girl, Aria." He bites his lip and watches me intently, as he continues to pleasure himself. "Now, spread your legs and get ready because I'm going to cum and it's going inside you," He warns, and I swallow back any thoughts of this being wrong and make a space for him. The ache inside me has turned into something different. It's not dull or heavy, it's wanting, and when the hand that was resting against the wall, quickly reaches under my thigh and lifts up my leg, my body burns as he pushes his cock into me in one, long thrust.

"You are so *fucking* tight," He growls into my ear through his teeth, as his cock pulses inside my sore, aching pussy.

"You take that." His fingertips clutch deep into my thigh as his heat spreads inside me, and I feel myself squeeze around him. He holds himself still, breathing heavily against my neck until he finds his calm again. Then he surprises me when he lifts up my other leg, taking me off my feet. The chain that holds me to the wall clatters as he spins our bodies and sits on the floor so I'm straddling his lap. He rests his against the wall and with one hand gripping onto my collar and the other holding my hip, he ensures I keep his still hard cock deep inside me. There is no regret or remorse in his eyes, just pure determination. And I can't describe what's happening inside my head. I feel possessed like my thoughts are no longer my own. Somehow I don't see a monster in this man who has taken me, I see something broken that I want to fix.

CHAPTER SEVEN

MATTEO

I stare at the girl and wonder what's going through her mind. My cock is still hard and seated deep inside her warm pussy, and there seems nothing more satisfying than knowing she's full of me. What's happening to me isn't healthy. She is making me weak, but it appears that her lack of resistance is helping my plans go smoothly and so there is little I will do about it.

"Matteo." I give her my name because I've decided I'd like to hear her say it.

"What?" She looks back at me with confusion on her face.

"I thought you should know the name of the man whose child you will carry." My fingers trace over her flat stomach and the thought of it swelling keeps my cock hard inside her.

"I want to know why—"

"Shhhh." I place a finger over her lips to silence her. "I won't tell you why, so don't ask." I don't know why I feel the need to keep it a secret from her. Maybe, I want to spare the girl from having to know what a cunt her father really is, or perhaps the fact that Fucchini's daughter takes my cock and what I fill her with, so willingly, is all the revenge I need.

Turns out Demitri was right, having her here will cause a war because I already know that I will never give her back.

An unfamiliar urge makes me take the girl in my arms and force her onto my chest, and when her arms automatically wrap around me, I feel a heat spread through my chest that doesn't belong there. I shouldn't be doing this, she is my prisoner. But it feels fulfilling and so I sit with her wrapped around my body for a little longer.

∼

Aria looks surprised the following evening when Lucas brings her up to the room, on my command. It's been sixteen hours since I fucked her in the basement, and I've decided that is plenty of time for her pussy to have recovered.

"A bath is ready for you." I gesture my head toward the bathroom door and she smiles at me like she's fucking grateful, as she steps through it and closes it after her. I'm about to get out of bed and re-open it, reminding her that she is not permitted to shut me out, but I get distracted when my phone rings.

"Well, it's happened," Demitri tells me, sounding smug.

"What has happened?" I don't have time for fucking guessing games.

"Fucchini is looking for her. A nationwide search has been started, he even has the cops involved on this one."

"Fuck." I scrub my hand over my face in frustration.

"It's not too late, you *could* give her back. We can easily scare her enough never to tell her father who took her." Demitri proves he has no idea what he's talking about.

"It is too late, we stick to the plan." I hang up the phone and storm straight into the bathroom. The girl looks way too relaxed for someone who's being held against her will as she lays in my bathtub, but that calm quickly turns to shock when I grip a fistful of her hair and force her to stand up.

"Do you want to marry Dennis Jefferson?" I ask, keeping my hold firm and watching her eyes brim with fear.

"No." She shakes her head against me, firmly.

"Your father is looking for you. So are the police. If they find you, you will have to marry that man and you will never see me again. Is that what you want?" I breathe like a fucking bull while I wait for her answer because, for some fucked-up reason, it feels really important.

"No," she whispers, with a much weaker shake of her head. Her puzzled expression suggests that even she doesn't understand her answer.

"Then come with me." I drag her out of the bath by her hair, into the bedroom and throw her soaked body onto the bed. My cock is already hard, it seems it always is when I'm near her, and as I spread her still-soapy legs and position myself between them, I let my thick tip rest between her pussy lips.

"I want you to call your father and tell him you're safe." I take my phone in my hand and take a leap of faith when I hand it to her. "You tell him that you are happy and that you will come home when you are ready."

"He'll trace the call," she warns, her hands shaking as she takes hold of it.

"It's a secure line. Now call him, and when he answers, I want you to put him on speaker phone." I tug at her wet hair until she nods her head, and her fingers fumble to dial his number into my keypad.

"Hello." Fucchini's voice comes through the speaker, and hearing it builds up an even more dangerous rage inside me.

"Daddy, it's me." Aria does a good job of sounding calm, especially considering that I have my cock stroking between her pussy lips.

"*Aria*, where the hell are you?" I hear the desperation in his voice, and when I look at her to remind her what to say, she bites her lip awkwardly.

"I'm safe, I just needed to get away for a while." I'm relieved when she does as she's told, how am I only just realizing what an impulsive, reckless thing putting a phone in her hand was to do? It's another reminder of what this girl does to me.

I reward Aria's obedience by slowly edging the tip of my cock inside her, and she makes an exasperated little breath as she closes her eyes, and tries to focus on her task.

"Aria, I have everyone looking for you! I've been worried sick. Your friends said you went for a walk and just disappeared."

"They were all sleeping. I called a water taxi to pick me up and take me from the island." She impresses me by thinking on her feet and it earns her another solid inch of cock.

"Daddy." She clutches the comforter in her free hand as I slowly roll my hips and stir myself inside her.

"Yes?"

"Please don't come looking for me. This is what I want." She quickly hangs up the phone and reaches her hand around my body, grabbing my ass in her hand and pushing for me to give her more.

"You're such a good girl," I give her my praise because I know she likes it. She's made me proud today and as I give her more of what she wants, I glide my fingers over her outstretched neck.

"Come for me, right now," I instruct, pushing every inch I have inside her and holding still. Her nails dig into my ass, as her wet skin slips against me. "Come on, I want you spilling that tight cunt all over my cock." I remain still, savoring the way her pussy throbs around me. She looks back at me with such hope and expectation that it starts to fucking hurt. I'm not the kind of man she should be looking at, like this. I took her without any consideration for how she would feel. I don't know what makes her so accepting of me, but it scares me, and men like me don't have the luxury of fear.

I turn my soft touch firm, clutching at her throat, and drilling my eyes into hers

"I told you to *fucking come!*" I hiss through my teeth, and when her hips start to buck wildly against my static body and she screams out my name, I immediately regret telling her it. It sounds exactly as I imagined it would. Like it belongs on her fucking lips.

Her body trembles and the way she clamps around me triggers my own release. I keep my cock rooted deep, letting my cum flood inside her, and I have to close my eyes and try to ignore that obsession I'm developing toward her. When I open them back up and see her looking up at me, her pert, little tits rising and falling as she catches her breath back, it hits me how dangerous that obsession is going to be.

CHAPTER EIGHT

ARIA

I've counted it as twenty-one days since I was kidnapped and, every day, I've been taken up to the room where he fucks me like a whore, then returns me to the basement like a prisoner. My feelings for him grow stronger, and yet he remains cold. I have a hunch that things are about to get a lot worse today when Tomas leads me into the room where I know he'll be waiting for me.

"Afternoon." Matteo places down his phone and dismisses Tomas with a flick of his fingers.

"I have something to tell you." I force the words out of my mouth, but he's already stepped up behind me, his hand wrapping around the back of my neck and forcing me to bend over the dressing table. Slowly, as the days have progressed, more furniture has been added to this room. There's a mirror in front of us now and I close my eyes to avoid looking in it as his hand slides into the front of my panties.

When I grab at his wrist to try and stop him, he forces me away with a confused look on his face.

"Since when did you start denying me?" He drags me back up by my throat so I'm taut with his body.

"I...I."

The fingers from his other hand slip between my folds and I watch the anger spread on his face, through our reflection, as he pulls them back out and examines the red streaks of blood on them.

"I was trying to tell you...but..." Why the fuck do I feel ashamed, and worst of all, disappointed? It only confirms how crazy being in this situation is making me.

Matteo doesn't hide his disappointment either and shocks me when his grip on my neck tightens and his blood-coated fingers swipe over my cheek, smearing it onto my skin.

"I guess we'll just have to try harder," he hisses at me spitefully, before backing away and leaving me alone. I grip the edge of the dresser in my hands, staring at my reflection, as suddenly the reality hits me.

Everything I feel for Matteo is one-sided. He has become my comfort, I crave him like a drug and I have no control over it. Perhaps it's my coping mechanism to get me through the situation I'm in.

When Tomas comes back into the room and tells me to follow him I wipe the tears from my eyes, and the blood from my face, before pushing myself off the dresser and going with him. Back to the confines of the basement, where I'm nothing more than a prisoner.

∾

It's been five days and I've stopped bleeding. I haven't seen Matteo since he left me in the bedroom that morning, and I hate him for ignoring me for all this time. I hate myself even more for actually missing him. He's kept me supplied with the products I've needed and allowed me into the room to bathe once a day, but there has been no sign of him and it's felt like a punishment. I realize now, why.

Matteo's only intention is to make me pregnant with his child. He can't do that while I'm bleeding and so, for the past few days, I've been insignificant to him. The door to the basement opens, and Tomas looks at me expectantly, so I get up on my feet with determination and follow him.

When I enter the room and see Matteo with his ass resting on the dresser and his legs crossed casually, I run at him and pull my hand back so I can slap the smug look off his face. He catches my wrist before I can make the connection and the smirk I saw when I first walked in here remains on his face.

"Missed me?" he questions, infuriating me even more.

I have no words for him, I want to cry but I won't, something tells me he'd fucking like it.

"Tomas tells me you have stopped bleeding." He releases me and heads towards the bed, rolling up the sleeves of his shirt before he pats the mattress for me to sit.

For the past two mornings, Tomas has asked me if my bleeding had stopped and it seems the word I sent him back with, earlier, has pleased his boss.

"I have," I confirm.

"Then we must get back to work straight away." He stands, waiting for me to go to him but I remain still, refusing to be the dog that heels after the way he's made me feel.

"You're mad at me." He shakes his head and rolls his eyes like it's an inconvenience. Coming toward me, he slides his hand through my hair and it feels too nice to stop him.

"Sweet, little Aria, as pretty as you look when you are angry, your emotions are pointless. They aren't going to change what will happen here, today. I'm still going to fuck you."

"And what if I don't want to be fucked today?" I swipe back

at him. The smile he responds with gives me a real urge to scratch it off his lips.

"And to think, I was going to do something nice for you." He shakes his head and shrugs, before crouching his body and lifting me up onto his shoulder. I protest as he carries me over to the bed and throws me onto the mattress. Giving me no time to try and break free, he grabs both wrists in one of his huge hands and pins them above my head.

I watch, restrained, as he unbuckles his belt with his free hand and I struggle against his firm hold when he tears open his slacks and takes out his cock.

"What are you going to do, rape me?" I snarl at him.

"You just tell me when to stop, Princess." He looks down at me calmly and waits for my reaction as the thick tip of his cock rubs against the lace of my panties. My arms stop moving and, despite my anger, my hips automatically fidget against him.

It's cruel, and devious, to use my emotions against me but I make myself a victim to it when I say nothing.

"That's what I thought." His finger hooks into the lace, dragging it to one side so we're flesh to flesh, and my stomach flips.

"In fact, I'm pretty sure that right now, I could have you beg me for it," he whispers, making me even wetter as his cock slowly slips between my folds, stroking that sweet spot and making me moan with pleasure and frustration at the same time.

"Do you wish to have me inside you, Aria?" he asks, tilting his head and enjoying every second of my suffering. I say nothing, just stare right back at him as I move my hips against him to get the friction I need.

"Answer the question, Aria." He looks down and spits at the tip of his cock while he continues to tease me with it.

"Yes," I admit when the emptiness inside me becomes intolerable.

"Then ask me nicely." His voice is soothing, and as much as I want to tear chunks out of him, my pussy is running my conscience right now. I take another glance down, seeing him huge and hard, pressed against me and craving to feel that sting of him pushing inside me. I know that letting him have what he wants will come with a price, but the desire in me is willing to pay it.

"Put it inside me, *please*." I manage, watching the smirk grow wider on his lips, as he drops to his knees and gives me his tongue instead. He takes his time, making agonizingly, slow licks as I buck against his face, proving that my need has overtaken any pride I stormed in here with.

"Desperation tastes so good on you." Matteo lifts his eyes up to me and watches me with great satisfaction as I cum all over his tongue. Before I have a chance to come down from the high, without any warning, he gets back on his feet and slams himself into me. I scream out in shock and Matteo grabs both my tits in his hands, through my bra, crushing them hard in his fist.

"It *looks* fucking good on you too," he tells me, fucking me hard and unforgivingly.

"Ask. Ask me to cum in this pretty, little pussy, Aria." He stares into my eyes and looks a little desperate himself. "Tell me you want it." I can deny him the words, but I can't deny the thoughts in my head. Sick and twisted as all this is, Matteo wanting to put his child inside me makes me feel special in a way I've never felt before.

"I want it," I tell him, meaning every word, despite wishing I didn't, and when his body stills, he groans loudly as he gives me what I want and empties inside me. His hands clutch my thighs tight around his hips as his seed fills my pussy, and as I look at the man, who I'm pretty sure is going to destroy me, I wonder what he would have to do to make me hate him.

CHAPTER NINE

MATTEO

"It's been a while since you checked in with your father, you should call him," I tell her, placing a cushion under her hips to ensure every drop of my cum stays inside her. Dr Fabier tells me that it's very rare for a woman to get pregnant within the first month of trying, but that doesn't stop me being disappointed that we were unsuccessful. I will do all I can to ensure that, this month, we do not fail.

"I think that would be a little awkward, right now." Aria looks down her body and giggles, proving that she's forgiven me for being absent these past few days. What she won't know, is that I suffered just as much as she did. I had to gain back some control and test myself. I needed some space away from her and all the feelings she puts inside me. Although, all it proved is that I'm every bit as weak as I thought I was. The amount of times I almost gave in and went to that basement, just so I could fuck her out of pure need, is embarrassing.

"I do recall the last time you spoke to him, my cock was actually inside you," I remind her, laying on the bed beside her and sliding my palm up her thigh so I can gather up the cum that's starting to leak out of her dripping, little hole, and push it back in.

"So, what was this nice thing you were going to do for me?" she asks, with that sweet smile back on her face.

"I'm not going to tell you, now." I shrug, and when she pouts, it takes every strength inside me not to press my lips over hers and kiss it away.

"You're cruel." She somehow manages to smile and scowl at the same time, and being laid with her, like this, makes it too easy to forget what this is...

This is vengeance, not the start of a love story.

"Stay here for a while. Relax. I'll have Tomas take you down to the basement in an hour." I clear my throat, as I pull my finger from inside her and stand back up.

"Don't leave, maybe we could talk for a while?" She props herself up on her elbows and looks up at me hopefully.

"I can't." I shake my head, quickly getting out of the room before the clever, little temptress actually has me giving in to her.

∽

I'm in my office eating my dinner alone, when Tomas opens the door and shows me the tray in his hands.

"She's not eating again, boss." He shrugs, making my pulse fucking tick.

"Put the plate there." I lower my eyes to my desk and he moves forward to do as I request.

"Now, go and get her," I order, barely able to believe my own words as he nods his head and disappears. I shouldn't play into the girl's games, they are dangerous. But I need her to be healthy, and being with her for just that little time today has reminded me how much I enjoy her company. Aria steps into my office a few minutes later, wearing the black lace underwear, I keep her supplied with, and looking all innocent and fucking timid.

"Sit," I command, pointing my head toward the chair on the other side of my desk. She smiles victoriously as she takes it, and makes my palm twitchy.

"Eat." I push the plate of food closer to her, trying not to give her too much of my attention. She gets quite enough of that. In fact, she's all I seem to think about these days.

We eat together in silence, and as much as I hate to admit it, it feels kind of comforting. I'm not usually a man who enjoys company, time with her seems to be the exception. When Aria places down her fork, I nod to show her that I'm impressed with her empty plate, then just as I'm about to dismiss her she blurts out the words she's been holding in since she came through the door.

"You made me feel used and I didn't like it," she admits, keeping her head held high. I can tell by the look on her face that her little confession has cost her some pride. "And yes, I know what this is. I'm not deluded. Or maybe I am. I don't know." Her brave act slips when she closes her eyes and shakes her head. "My feelings are so confusing, sometimes I just want to tear them out of my head."

I've never related more to anything in my life, but I won't admit that to her. I show her far too much weakness as it is, and I'm getting no pleasure out of her distress, which makes me wonder what the hell is happening to me.

"I hate being down in that basement and knowing you're up here. I get so lonely, and I...I." I don't know if she can't get her words out or if she's scared to. "What's going to happen to me if I *do* give you a child? Do you plan to keep me down there forever?"

I feel my brow crease as I take in what she says. Foolish as it sounds, I never thought that far ahead. In fact, I never thought this through at all. I didn't expect to feel the way I do about her, and now, I'm all out of fucking answers.

I stare back at her blankly, terrified of what I actually want to tell her.

"Matteo, I need you to answer me. I'm scared."

Fuck, why does that hurt to hear? I *wanted* her fear. I *wanted* her pain and now, it feels like a weapon she can use against me.

"Come with me." I stand up and take her hand in mine, dragging her up the stairs and cursing myself for going against all my better judgment.

I open the door to the room I always fuck her in and nod for her to go inside.

"You sleep in here from now on," I keep my voice stern. "You do not leave this room without my permission and you will not try to escape." I drag her over to the barred windows and roughly grab the back of her hair, forcing her to look out of it toward the guard I have on the back door.

"See that dog, he's got? She's trained to chase and attack." I lean close enough for my lips to touch her ear. "You are far too pretty to have your face ripped off," I whisper before releasing her and quickly heading for the door. I've shown the girl enough kindness for one night.

"Matteo!" She calls my name out desperately, and when I turn around and see the cute smile on her face, the warmth it puts in my chest makes me want to tear it open and drag it back out.

"Thank you," she whispers before I spin back around and get the fuck out of there.

I head straight toward my own room and slam the door behind me. I stare at myself in the full-length mirror and barely recognise myself. Not much may have changed on the outside, but on the inside, I feel like I've been possessed. It's unnerving, it's unfamiliar, and I punch my fist at the man looking back at me because it was *not* part of the fucking plan.

CHAPTER TEN

ARIA

Matteo wasn't wrong when he said we would be trying harder. I've been sleeping in this room for four days now and every day he has come to me more than once.

Tonight is his third time visiting me today, and as he pulls out of me and positions another cushion under my hips, he lays down beside me and catches his breath.

"Have you thought about what's going to happen when this baby gets here?" I ask, talking as if one already exists. I spend a lot of time by myself these days and it's given me the opportunity to think about all this. My father is not a forgiving man. If he finds out where I am, he will not allow Matteo to keep me, or my child.

Matteo doesn't answer my question, he just sighs as he stares at the ceiling with his hands behind his head. I like that he doesn't rush off after fucking me, anymore. The time we spend like this may be short but I enjoy it, even if it is always silent.

"My father will eventually find out where I am, and when he does he will take me and—"

"No one is taking you!" Matteo quickly slams his hand over

my mouth, looking furious at the idea. "You belong to *me* now. Do you really think I'm scared of your father?" His eyes narrow fiercely.

"Your father is a pussy, Aria, he doesn't fight like a man."

"And this is you fighting like a man?" I question him, wondering what the hell goes through this guy's head.

"No, this is me playing your father at his own game," he admits, putting a real sour taste in my mouth.

"What if I don't want to be part of that game?" I stare at him hard and let him see my hurt. I don't know if Matteo has always been closed off to emotion, and perhaps there's a chance I could draw on some, now.

"That is just the way of it. We don't get to choose what we are born into, Aria, and you were born into this life, just like I was."

"Not our child. We get to decide that. Or at least you do. Do *you* really want to bring a child into this life?"

"You shouldn't question me." Matteo gets off the bed and heads for the chair, where his pants are. "It is not your job to question me. I know what I'm doing."

"You can't keep me, Matteo." I kneel up on the mattress and he immediately comes for me, reaching behind my legs and pulling them from under me so I fall back onto my back.

"Don't underestimate me." Pulling my legs together, he holds them up over one of his shoulders. Making sure that the load, he just fucked into me, doesn't seep out.

I've made him mad, I can tell by the tension in his fingers and the sternness in his eyes as he frowns down at me.

"What happens once the child is born, is for me to worry about," he tells me.

"And what about me, what will you do with me, Matteo? Because I don't want to go back." I shake my head at him, as tears fill my eyes and the emotions inside me outdo my ability to be brave. "I don't want to marry Dennis Jefferson."

The anger on Matteo's face softens as he studies me, and suddenly he seems confused.

"I don't know what's happening to me, I don't know when this became something I wanted, but the thought of going back to the way things were, breaks my heart," I try to explain, but it all comes out wrong and makes me sound completely at his mercy.

"You'd rather be my prisoner than go back to your family?" He narrows his eyes at me, suspiciously.

"I'm just as much of a prisoner there, as I am here. Do you know why me and my so-called friends were on that island, the day your men took me?"

The look on Matteo's face is unreadable as his strong arm clutches around my legs that are elevated over his shoulders.

"My dad promised me a trip away before he gave me to Jefferson. That was supposed to be me saying goodbye to them all because he knew, that once I became that man's wife, that my life would be over. Those people weren't even real friends, they were sons and daughters of men he's felt the need to impress. I have been my father's bargaining tool since the day I was born. Over the years I have been promised to five different men, and I was only seven when he promised me to the first. I never saw a way out of that before, and I never had the hope to look for one."

"And you think this is it?" Matteo asks, separating my legs and sliding his body between them.

"It feels like a better offer than Dennis Jefferson." I smile up at him despite my sadness, but he doesn't return it, he does something far more shocking. He kisses me, on the lips, slowly and almost passionately. His hand moves between our bodies so he can guide his cock back inside me again, and when I feel him slowly fill me, I anchor my legs around his hips and kiss him right back.

"You're already so full of my cum. You're fucking soaking," he breathes against my mouth.

"I want more of it." I give up on telling myself this is wrong. The heart wants what it wants and, as nasty and vicious as this man can be, mine has attached itself to his black, broken one.

"Fuck, Aria!" His thrusts are much softer than usual, and there's something different in the way he looks at me. Something that feels so wonderful, I could cry.

"I'll never let anyone take you. You're mine now, okay?" he assures me. Holding my thighs tight around him as he fucks me slowly, stirring more emotions inside me that I don't know how to deal with, I feel my orgasm start to build and wonder if that is what has me so defenseless to this man. I crave it when he's not around, he controls when he lets me have it and when he does, it feels like nothing else on the earth matters.

I grip his hair in my hands and breathe into his ear as I come, and he keeps the pace steady. Continuing to push in and out of me in long, slow strokes that prolongs my orgasm for way longer than usual. His fingers clasp around my jaw and pull me back so his eyes have my attention.

"I promise, Dennis Jefferson will never lay a hand on you," he growls as he continues feeding himself into me.

"You're mine," he repeats, releasing my face and dropping his head into my shoulders, groaning as he comes again. I feel the weight of his body, heavy on top of me, and stroke my fingers through his hair as we breathe in sequence and our heartbeats regulate.

"Sleep now, Aria. You have nothing to fear." He keeps himself deep inside me, reaching back and pulling the comforter over us both so we can sleep.

CHAPTER ELEVEN

MATTEO

I left her sleeping, with her hair feathered out over the pillow like an angel, and her pussy full of my cum. I've never fallen asleep beside a woman before, let alone with my cock still inside one. I liked how it felt, and I've come to the realization that with her, I've been allowing myself far too many pleasures.

Tonight, I need to remind myself of who I am. And I know just how to do it, effectively.

My leather-gloved hand grips tight around the steering wheel as I stare across the street into Dennis Jefferson's mansion. The knots twist my stomach when I think about him and her, together. Aria is young, she has a whole life ahead of her and her father can't possibly love her if he was thinking of marrying her off to this rotting corpse of a man.

Power would have been his only motive. Dennis Jefferson plans to run for senator next year, and having a man like him in your pocket would be beneficial to Fucchini.

It's taken me three hours to drive here, and in that time I've thought about all the ways I could kill him. I made Aria a promise tonight, one that I won't break. I have to be sure that if something goes wrong and Aria ends up in the hands of her father again, marrying Dennis Jefferson will not be an option.

It's been years since I did something like this, alone. Usually, men are brought to me, they get to kneel at my feet and beg for their mercy before I kill them. But this is different. I want to do this by myself. I want to do this for her.

I check my watch, it's late, way past midnight, and I'm sure the old man will be sleeping soundly in his bed. So, getting out of the car, I make my way across the street and like a teenage boy, I scale the fence to his backyard. When we were younger, me and Demitri had a lot to prove to our fathers. I may have been Angelo Romano's only son and heir, but my dad made it very clear he wouldn't leave his empire to someone incompetent. To be a successful Romano you have to work your way from the ground up. I'm thankful to him for that tonight when I take the lock picker out of my back pocket and hold the torch between my teeth, as I pick the lock of Jefferson's back door.

I prove I haven't lost my touch when it opens a few seconds later, and then quietly let myself in and creep through his living room.

The place is impressive, as I imagined it would be, and I try to imagine it being Aria's home. These days the only space I can imagine her being in is mine. I'm not a fool, I know in order to keep her the way I want to, I will have to change my plan. I can't keep her hidden forever, even if I wanted to. But I will not give her up. The thought of her being here has the leather of my gloves creasing when I fist my hands. Slowly, I take the stairs up to the second floor looking for the man who Fucchini intended to be his daughter's husband.

The floorboards creak when I get to the top and after

carefully opening the first door I come to, I find the room empty. I check behind three more doors before I find him sleeping in his bed, snoring like a wild boar with his huge gut protruding from under the covers.

I step forward until I'm standing beside him. The old fucker continues to snore, his mouth hanging open and his double chin wobbling. Then quietly I open the top drawer of his nightstand and remove the gun I find there, sliding it into the back of my slacks.

I watch him for a while before I turn on the bedside lamp, and slap the side of his face to wake him up. He snorts as he startles awake, and his shock quickly turns to fear when he sees me.

"What...? What is this?"

"Good evening, Mr Jefferson," I speak calmly as I take the knife from my belt and twist the handle in my palm.

"Get out of my home!" He reaches for his drawer and I take his arm in my hand, twisting it awkwardly.

"I'm here to ask, why you wish to marry Aria Fucchini?"

I ignore him and get straight to the point. I want to be back home before dawn so I can stir his fiancée awake with my cock.

"That is none of your business." He shakes his head and squints his eyes as he studies me closer.

"Wait... I know who you are. You're Matteo Romano."

"Correct. Now, answer my question."

When Jefferson struggles, I press the blade of my knife under his chin to keep him right where he is.

"Her...her father thought it would be a good fit." His voice trembles as he looks down his nose at the blade. It's glistening from the moonlight coming through his window, and his sweat is already wetting it.

"A good fit? You're old enough to be her *grandfather*."

"I also have many connections at the docks. The girl was

an..." He rubs his lips together hungrily, "...an enticing offer, but if you want to place something on the table, yourself, we could come to an arrangement."

"Something like your life?" I press the blade deeper into his flesh, piercing the skin enough to make a dent.

"I didn't come here to make you an offer, old man." I make sure my smile is the last one he sees when I slice the blade neatly across his throat, then I stand back so I can watch the horror on his face as he clutches the open wound with his hands and the blood pours through his fingers. It's a strange kind of satisfaction I get from watching him die, different to the one I usually get.

Once his skin is pale, and his eyes are soulless, I leave him in a pool of his own blood and head back to the only person who seems to matter.

~

When I arrive home, instead of going to my room like I should, I go to hers. I take off my clothes and put them in the trash bag I got from the kitchen on my way up, screwing it in a ball and hiding it behind the curtain. Then, heading for her bathroom, I get in the shower and wash the blood from my body before I join her back in bed. She fidgets as I get under the covers, naturally curling her body into mine and placing her head against my chest, and I hold my hand over it to keep it there because I like the way it feels. The heaviness of whatever this is hits me when I realize that tonight is only scratching the surface on how far I'd go to keep her. I wrap my arm around her waist and let my fingers stretch across her stomach, wondering if my seed has taken hold inside her, yet. Aria is going to look so fucking beautiful when her stomach swells with our child. So beautiful that it makes me want to disturb her from her sleep to increase the chances of it happening sooner, rather than later. I manage to hold off, though. I have to take care of her now. She is my responsibility and I will make sure her body remains healthy. I gently kiss the top of her head before resting my chin on it and getting some sleep myself.

CHAPTER TWELVE

ARIA

I wake up, shocked to find Matteo beside me. His arms are wrapped tightly around my body, clutching to me as if he's worried I'll run away. The scary thing about all this is the fact I know I won't. I slowly untangle myself and get out of bed so I can use the toilet and when I open the curtains I notice a black bag on the floor behind them. Taking a peek inside I see what looks like a balled-up suit, and a pair of black leather gloves. I have no idea why they are here but I leave them where I found them so I can head to the bathroom.

I brush my teeth before I go back to him, and when I step through the door his eyes are open and staring at me like I'm in trouble.

"What did I do?" I shrug my shoulders.

"Nothing. I'm allowed to look at you, aren't I?" He raises his eyebrows as I slowly move towards him and climb back onto the bed.

"I don't know, you make the rules. Are you?" I tease, straddling his body with mine. When he reaches his hand up to frame my cheek, his touch seems almost tender.

"Yes." He stares into my eyes so deeply I feel them burn,

and when his cock presses hard between my legs, I have to resist the temptation to rub myself against it.

"You are going to stop me from getting any work done, today," he warns, dropping his eyes to look between us.

"Did you have something important to do?" I lick my finger and slowly trace it around the thick head of his shaft.

"Nothing more important than this." He takes both my hips in his hands and guides me on top of him. While I reach between us and line him up with my entrance, not only am I encouraging this, but I desperately want it.

I have no idea what Matteo's intentions are once he gets me pregnant, but I've noticed a shift in his behavior, and I've never felt more alive than I do right now. Yes, he's dangerous, but I was raised amongst danger and I feel safe with him, despite how I got here.

"That's right, you steer my cock into your pussy." His teeth graze over his bottom lip as he watches me slide myself over his tip. It makes me feel in control like I'm the one pleasuring him, and I like it. Slowly, I sit on his cock, taking it all the way and making us both moan from how good it feels.

"Nothing feels better than this," he whispers, clutching at my hips as I grind them against his body, stirring his cock inside me and feeling my pulse quicken. I rest my palms on his chest for leverage as I move up and down his long, thick shaft and he watches me intently as I do it, his stare penetrating me almost as deep as his cock is. I don't let myself think about how fucked up this situation is, or the damage it will do to me. I do what he told me to, and I take from him what I need.

I've given up caring that I'm not protected too, his obsession with knocking me up seems almost infectious, because sick as it sounds, I like the idea of being bound to him for life. I *want* to be the cause of his happiness and I want something of his growing inside me.

"What are you thinking, Princess?" He tilts his head to one side as his hand travels up my body and wraps around one of my tits.

My head shakes because I refuse to tell him. I can't, it sounds too ridiculous. I don't know Matteo's reasons for wanting this, he refuses to tell me, but mine feel weak and childish, so I'll keep them to myself.

"Tell me," he orders, gripping the hair at my nape and tugging it till a slither of pain slices down my spine. The kind of pain that turns my nipples even harder and makes my clit throb.

"I'm... I'm." I keep myself bouncing on his cock and when the hand, still holding my hip, stills me and holds me firm, he focuses his narrow eyes on me in warning.

"Tell me," he growls through his teeth.

"I...I'm thinking, how much I want your cum," I blurt out the words, desperate to feel that friction again, and I can see my words have pleased him by the tiny smile that hitches up his lips.

"Tell me more." He licks his lips and flicks his eyes between mine and where we're joined.

"I want everything you've promised to give me," I confess, throwing my head back and savoring how good it feels when he guides my hips to start moving again. Having him inside me at this angle makes me feel so full it almost hurts, and although the grip he has on my hair reminds me he's in control again, I realize that's the way I want it.

"I want you to give me all your cum. I want to have your baby inside me," I manage.

"Keep talking like that, and I'll be filling you before you get off yourself," he warns.

"I don't care." Defying the hold he's keeping me steady with, I bounce harder on his cock.

"I'm gonna fuck you so full it will be spilling out of you for days." He loses control, slamming his hips up from under me and making my body shudder with pleasure. "You better come fast, Princess, because it's coming." He wets his thumb with his tongue before pressing it against my clit, massaging my sensitive flesh with just the right pressure to bring me up to his level.

"Matteo," I whisper his name, as I get closer and closer.

"I like it when you say my name." He forces the words out of his mouth like they hurt him to admit, and if I wasn't so close to having a mind-shattering orgasm, I'd smile at the victory.

"You ready?" he checks, and when I nod my head, the fingers resting on my hips dig deep into my flesh as he holds me tight against his body and offloads inside me. He moans with pleasure as he pumps me full of his cum and that, along with the sensation of his thumb still working my clit, gets me right there with him.

The pair of us are a breathless, throbbing mess as we wind back down, and when his cock stops pulsing inside me and I go to move, Matteo holds me firm.

"No. You stay like that." Reaching up he gently pushes the hair, that's stuck to my face, behind my ear so he can stroke my cheek with his thumb.

"You look so fucking perfect like this." He drags me down onto his lips and kisses me hard.

"I don't want to be your prisoner anymore, Matteo, I just want to be yours." My words come out needy and desperate, but I don't care. I need him to know that I submit to him and that I would never run.

"You *are* mine," he promises. "Now, lay here on my chest and keep my cock deep inside you. I want to make sure you're knocked up this time."

CHAPTER THIRTEEN

MATTEO

I text Demitri and tell him I'm taking the day off. I can't remember the last time I did it, but after Aria made her confession to me this morning, I want to stay close to her. We fall back to sleep for a few hours, then we wake up and go downstairs for a mid-morning breakfast, hand in hand, like a real couple. My best friend has a very disturbed look on his face when he sees us.

"Matteo, I must talk with you." He follows us into the dining room and watches as I pull out Aria's chair for her. The way his eyes flick over her barely-covered body makes me decide that from now on she needs to start wearing much more than what I provide her with when she is downstairs. I don't want the others looking at what's mine.

"Matteo." He speaks up again like I didn't hear him the first time.

"Then talk." I take Aria's plate and start to load it with the things I want her to eat. Then smile at her as I place it back in front of her.

"Well, come on, what is so important? You may speak in front of her." I look to Demitri for an explanation.

"Dennis Jefferson was found dead at his home this morning," he informs me, flicking his eyes between us and waiting for a reaction.

"I know, I was the one who killed him," I confess, hearing the spoon, Aria was eating her grapefruit with, clatter against her plate.

"You...You did *what?*" She stares back at me horrified.

"I made you a promise and I saw it through." I shrug simply.

"Matteo, you didn't tell me the plan..." Demitri interrupts and I stop him going any further into this by raising my hand.

"There *was* no plan, it was a spur-of-the-moment decision," I explain.

"I feel sick." Aria's skin suddenly turns pale and her delicate little hand covers her mouth.

Hearing this any other time would make me hopeful, but I know it's not the condition she may be in that's causing it. She's disgusted by my actions.

I can see from the look on his face that Demitri doesn't agree much with them, himself.

"May I be excused?" She looks up from the table at me, and I see the tears filling her eyes. The unfamiliar tug I feel in my chest has me nodding my head at her, and she gets up and practically runs to the door. I gesture my head to Ludo to follow after her.

"Matteo, you are scaring me with your rash decisions." Demitri takes up the seat she just vacated and looks at me. "Did you do a clean job? It's been a while since you–"

"Since I took a field trip." I decide to finish his sentence for him. "Having men brought to me has become boring, besides, I wanted to do this one myself. He was going to marry her, as part of a deal with Fucchini. He would never have made her happy." I reach across the table to get some bacon for myself.

"And you think you can? Here, like this, forcing her to become pregnant with your child and keeping her like a prisoner?" Demitri scoffs a laugh at me that makes me want to slit his throat too.

"Does it sound so crazy?" I raise my shoulders again and pout.

"Yes, Matteo, it sounds *fucking* crazy. As soon as Fucchini knows where she is, he will come for her. He will bring men and there will be a war."

"I'm figuring that out," I admit, trying not to fidget uncomfortably in my chair. Truth is, I have no idea what to do, yet.

"This isn't about vengeance anymore, is it, Matteo?" My best friend looks at me sternly, daring me to lie to him.

"I don't know what it's about, anymore. I just know that I can't lose her." I leave him to make of that what he wants, taking the plate Aria left behind and going to find her.

Ludo tells me she went back to her room, so that's where I head and I find her lying on the bed, with a blank look on her pretty, little face.

"You're mad at me," I tell her, placing the plate beside her like it's some kind of peace offering. Though, I make no apologies for what I did.

"Here, you can be mad and eat at the same time."

She surprises me by being compliant, picking up the plate and popping one of the strawberries between her pouty lips.

"Aria, I had to kil–"

"Don't you *dare!*" she interrupts. "Don't tell me you had to kill that man because of a promise you made to me."

"Okay, I won't say that, but I will tell you this. Me taking you, and keeping you here, comes with a risk. Until I have a better plan, your father could come and try to take you at any time. The only way he could succeed in that is to kill me, and if he did, there would have been nothing stopping him from making you marry that man. I wasn't going to allow it."

"You think my dad will find me?" The angry look on her face suddenly turns into worry and it makes my cold heart miss a fucking beat.

"I can't keep you hidden forever, Princess." I slowly take a seat on the mattress beside her, running my hand over her smooth thigh.

"It would be no life for you, or our child, to keep you locked away."

"I told you, I don't want to go back," she tells me with wide, worried eyes, that make me feel so fucking weak, it's scary.

"I know, and I will find a way for this to work out. I promise." I offer her a reassuring smile and she says nothing, just looks down to the edge of the pillow, that she's fiddling with in her hand.

"I think there's something wrong with me." She blushes when she eventually looks back up.

"What?" Concern punches me straight in the gut as I glance her over.

"I shouldn't want all this, what you did, what we're doing here is wrong. You took me against my will, and yet in my head, you're a savior."

"I think I'd prefer to be your savior than a monster," I tell her, letting a satisfied smile show on my face.

"I mean it, Matteo. I have no idea what's come over me. I should be resisting you and yet…"

"Shhhhh. You are thinking too much on this. I will confess something to you." I take the pillow from her hand and toss it to the floor, then holding both her hands in mine, I prepare to give up a little more than I should.

"I never intended on this happening," I admit watching her head shake in confusion.

"Matteo, just tell me why." She's begging now and it looks so pretty, I almost wish I *could* tell her. Technically there is no reason that I couldn't, but for some reason, I feel I need to protect her from the truth.

"Promise me you will not try to run." I ignore her question and focus on something else.

"And have my face ripped off by one of your dogs?" She looks up at me, managing a sarcastic smile.

"I'm being serious, give me your word and I will give you something in return."

She looks back at me, with intrigue.

"You have my word," she whispers, with a serious look on her face and determination in her eyes.

"This house is now your home, not your prison. You are free to roam it as you like." I watch her mouth drop open, for the second time today.

"And the gardens?" she checks.

"You are not to go outside alone. If you wish to take some air, I will permit it as long as myself, or a guard, are with you."

"Will you take a walk with me, now?" she stares back at me hopefully, seeming to have forgotten all about her original question.

"I'd like that very much." I stand up and offer her my hand "But I'm getting you a shirt first." I drag her onto her feet and kiss her lips because I've come to realize that this girl doesn't just make me feel weak, she makes me feel a little hopeful too.

CHAPTER FOURTEEN

ARIA

"Aria, it's time to come home. I'm getting worried. Dennis is dead. He was murdered." My father scolds me, like a child, down the phone while Matteo lies beside me, drawing circles around my tummy button and listening intently.

"I saw it on the news," I admit. Dennis' murder has been headline news, and my biggest concern being that Matteo gets found out, has made me realize how twisted I've become.

"Enough is enough now, Aria! You can't expect me to be okay with you disappearing. It's been almost two months. I demand you tell me where you are!" He sounds beyond angry and yet, I don't fear him anymore. I draw strength from Matteo and the way he looks so proud of me.

"I'm not expecting you to be okay with it. But I also won't be obeying your commands, anymore. I'm not a little girl, and I'm not a bargaining tool. I'm pleased Dennis is dead."

"*Aria!*" Father sounds as angry, as he is horrified.

"I need to go, I called because I didn't want you worrying about me."

"Don't hang up. Please. Let me send you some money. Just tell me where to send it."

"I don't need money, Father. I have everything I need. I love you." I hang up the phone and pass it back to Matteo and after he checks it's disconnected he places it on the nightstand behind him.

"You should sleep, you're looking tired." He gets up from the bed and starts to get dressed.

"Well, you *have* fucked me on every surface of the house this past week," I remind him, trying my best not to yawn. I don't want our evening to be over yet.

"Come back to bed, I want to talk." I tap the mattress beside me and look up at him hopefully. Me and Matteo have become very familiar with each other over the past few weeks, physically, but we don't speak much. I want to know him better, so much about him intrigues me.

"Talk about what?" He looks puzzled but still abandons the job of buttoning up his shirt so he can rest back on the bed beside me. I move to be closer to him, just lately it seems the only time I feel satisfied.

"I don't know anything about you. I want to know you better." I shrug.

"You don't want to know me," Matteo laughs to himself sadly, his fingers playing with a loose strand of my hair before he tucks it behind my ear. I love how it feels when he's gentle, almost as much as I do when he's rough.

"Why would you think that?" I stare back at him in confusion. It seems that under the surface, Matteo isn't as confident as he makes himself out to be.

"I'm a selfish man, Aria, the fact you're here proves that." He goes to move away again but I place my hand over his just in time to stop him.

"I don't think that's true. I believe you can be kind."

"That's because you have good in your heart, the kind of good that, given time, I will destroy." I watch him swallow the lump in his throat as his eyes move away from mine, to avoid contact.

"Have you ever been in love before?" I ask, desperate to know if his reason for being so cold stems from him getting hurt.

"I'm not capable of love," he answers sharply.

"So, you will not love our child?" The thought hurts me, even though there is no evidence, yet, of me being pregnant. I'm starting to believe it would be impossible for me not to be, though.

"That's different."

"How is it different? You shouldn't bring a child into the world unless you intend to love it." I can see this heading towards a disagreement, which is a bad idea, but I will not sit quietly on the subject. Matteo may have taken my freedom and my sanity, but I won't have him break my spirit.

"I want to carry on my family name, Aria. You were raised in this life, you must understand how important that is."

"I don't, for me, a child should be loved and adored, not created to be an heir."

"And what about you, will *you* love our child? Even though it will be mine." Matteo does what he's good at and turns my question around.

"Of course, I will, that's why I'm so scared."

"Scared?" He narrows his eyes at me.

"Of what I will become after I've given you what you want. This isn't a relationship, Matteo, you said yourself, this is me giving you what you want. Once you have it, what will be my purpose? To nurse your child, to take care of it when you aren't raising it to rule your empire?"

Suddenly, I'm feeling overwhelmed by my own questions.

"I told you, you are mine now." He shakes his head and I sense him becoming agitated.

"You can't keep me hidden forever, you said that yourself. Even if you could, I'd eventually try to run," I warn.

"To where? Your father?" He looks back at me mockingly, his body overpowering mine as he clambers over me, and I see that cruel glint in his eyes that I've been seeing less and less, lately.

"I don't pretend to understand you, Aria. I never expected this. You say you won't obey your father anymore, and yet, you are so content to obey me. You are willing and far too accepting. I still don't know if this is part of a game you're playing. But what I do know is this..." His hand wraps around my throat and his fingers tense.

"You will never be free of me. You've become a fucking curse, but your *my* curse. Don't you forget that." His grip remains firm and almost choking, yet the kiss he places on my forehead is so delicate, I barely feel it.

"Sleep now, Aria. You need your rest." He gets up from the bed and leaves me.

CHAPTER FIFTEEN

MATTEO

I leave her and head straight to my office, pouring myself something strong and feeling the frustration prickle my veins. Does she think I haven't been asking myself the same fucking questions that are going around in her head? It's *all* I think about, and I know the answers. I just don't know how to make them possible. When Thalia first told me she was pregnant with my child, I wasn't happy. I'd always known I would need to make a family someday but I was nowhere near ready. More importantly, *I* wanted to choose the woman I made one with. Thalia was a nice enough girl to fuck, we had our fun, but I didn't want to marry her. It had taken me some time to come to terms with it, I started to appreciate what she would be giving me, and in return, I wanted to give her a happy life. I would have tried to love her. Having them taken from me was a reminder of the danger that my love can bring, and although I know I could easily let myself fall for the girl upstairs, I can't.

Why does she have to make that so fucking hard?

I scrub my face and look out the window into the black. Why could I not have hated her? It would have been so much easier to fuck my child into her, and not give a shit about what happened to her once I had what I wanted. My revenge on Fucchini would have been the broken wreck I sent her back to him in, and when he came for his grandchild I would have killed him.

Now, I need a new plan because there is no way I could ever hurt the perfect, little creature sleeping upstairs who could potentially already be carrying my child.

I have a few more drinks and try to focus on some work, but everything in my head seems so complicated. Demitri has been taking care of things while I've been focusing on the girl. I already know I've been spending far too much time with her and not enough time on business. Distribution is moving fast, and it won't be long before we run out of supply. If my Columbian contact doesn't come through for me soon, I'll have to be looking elsewhere and I haven't got the time, or the energy, to be making connections right now.

I hear the faint knock on my door and when it slowly creaks open without my permission, I stand up ready to yell at whoever thinks they can disturb me. I manage to hold my tongue when Aria's head pops around the door, and she smiles at me, nervously.

"Sorry, am I interrupting something?" She bites that bottom fucking lip and when I shake my head she steps all the way inside.

"I couldn't sleep and you said I could have free reign around the house, now," she reminds me, stepping closer to my desk.

Instead of taking the seat opposite, she walks round it so she's standing beside me. My hand automatically wraps around her waist, dragging her sideways so she's standing in front of me.

"I made you mad, I didn't mean to do that," she whispers, running her fingers through my hair in that way that sends me fucking wild.

"You only asked me questions. Questions you deserve the answer to. And I will give them to you..." I look up at her, "... just as soon as I figure them out for myself." I sound so weak I don't recognise my own voice.

"I'm really confused about my feelings. I don't know why you want this so badly from me, and I sure as hell don't know why I want to give it to you. But, if we *do* make a child together, I need you to promise that you will never take it away from me." She holds the crook of her finger under my chin to ensure I look into her eyes. They are brimming with tears, and fear, which only confirms what an excellent mother she is going to make.

"I can promise you that." I nod my head and mean every word I fucking say. Somewhere, between letting her in my head and bringing her up from the basement, I've had to accept that having a child with her wouldn't be enough. The way she gives herself to me feels like a gift and I won't take that for granted.

"Why are you restless?" I slide my fingertips under the nightdress she's wearing, letting them skim the inside of her thigh.

"I don't like upsetting you. It's not everyone's kink to cause someone pain." She tips her head and smiles at me sassily, and although it makes me want to punish her, I can't help but like it.

"Turn around," I instruct, standing up myself and loosening my slacks. The excited little look she gives me over her shoulder, as she does what I ask, makes my cock grow even harder.

"Now, reach all the way over my desk and grip the other

side." I press my palm into her back, urging her forward, while my other hand slides her silk nightdress over her hips. I pause when I realize she's not wearing anything underneath it.

"I don't like the idea of you not wearing panties around my guards." I lean over her body and breathe into her ear. "Now, would you like me to fuck you like this?"

"Yes, please," she manages, her knuckles turning white as she grips the edge of my desk with her fingers.

"Tell me what else you want, Aria." I gently slide my hand between her legs and start working her with my finger. Her pussy is already wet and ready for me. Perfect for breeding.

"Your cum," she whispers, already getting off on the way I touch her.

"And where do you want my cum?" I slip two fingers into her tight, drenched hole and feel her throb around them.

"Inside me, *deep* inside me." She reaches her arms back behind her and grabs my hair, allowing my free hand access to roam all over the front of her body. I slide it up under the silk of her nightdress, between her tits, before I clasp her throat with my fingers.

"You sound so sweet, begging me to fill you. Tell me more. Tell me again how badly you want my child growing inside you."

"Matteo." She rolls her head back and moans when I replace my fingers with my cock.

"I...I want...please." She can barely get her words out and it puts a satisfied smile on my face as I push my fingers into her mouth so she can taste herself on them.

"Suck," I command. "Suck me with your mouth, and your cunt, at the same time." My grip on her throat gets tighter as I thrust into her, hard and fast, over and over again until she screams my name and her body stiffens.

"I'm gonna come, get ready to squeeze me tight inside you.

I don't want your pussy to waste a single fucking drop of what I give you. Do you understand?"

Aria nods and I slam my hips hard into hers one last time. My cock pulses inside her and, using the hand I have around her throat, I raise her body up from my desk and hold it flush to mine. I'm as deep inside her as I can get now; and feeling her walls penetrate around me, as I fill her tight, little pussy full, has my head spinning.

"*Fuck!*" My teeth sink into her shoulder and my fingers grasp at her hot, sticky flesh while we both catch our breaths. I manage to keep my cock inside her as I pull her back with me and rest on my chair.

"Put your legs up on my desk," I instruct, grabbing her thighs and lifting her shaky legs so they're spread out in front of us. I need to keep my cum inside her for as long as possible. She's due a period soon and I'm determined to ensure it doesn't come.

"This feels like a bad idea," she reaches behind her to wrap her arms around my neck, sitting with my cock still inside her and her legs elevated and spread over my desk.

"All good things come from bad ideas, Princess....that's what got you here in the first place." I gently slide my hand over her, soon-to-be, swollen stomach; nipping at her ear and feeling her pussy spasm around my cock.

CHAPTER SIXTEEN

ARIA

It's late morning when I wake up, and as the sun creeps through the window and warms my face, I smile to myself.

I can't pinpoint when everything changed, but what I do know is that nothing can ever go back to being normal. Is it wrong that I don't miss my father? That the only person I want to be around is Matteo? Even if it is, I don't think I care. I like the idea of the life he has planned for us.

The door knocks and when I call whoever it is in, Demitri smiles at me politely, as he places a tray of food on the bed.

"So, you're my servant, as well as my protector, now?" I sit up, making sure I'm covered by the blanket as I examine what's been sent up for me.

"Matteo figured you might want to stay in bed today, he's had to leave town. He will be back tomorrow evening."

"He never told me." I frown when I realize how much that hurts.

"You will learn that Matteo can be spontaneous." He widens his eyes and prepares to leave.

"Wait." I stop him. "What else can you tell me about Matteo?" I doubt he'll give me much of an answer. I know, from being the daughter of a Mafia boss, that men like Demitri earn their positions from loyalty.

"I can tell you not to fall in love with him, but I think it's a little late for that." A faint smile pulls on his stern lips.

"I'm not…I can't." I shake my head, though the little voice inside my head tells me that he's right.

"What do you think he will do when my father finds out where I am and tries to take me back?" I ask when those unwanted niggles start to override my happiness.

"I think he will do whatever it takes to keep you, and you need to be prepared for that." Any trace of a smile has disappeared from his face.

"I want to know what my father did," I tell him.

"Then you will have to ask Matteo, on his return." Demitri leaves before I can ask him any more questions; I breathe out an exasperated breath and let myself fall back onto my pillow.

There has to be a way for me to fix this. As far as my father is concerned, I left the island of my own free will. He doesn't know how me and Matteo came to be.

Just thinking about it all makes my head hurt, is it too much to ask that, maybe, what me and Matteo have could be accepted by my father? Even if it could, I fear Matteo's hate for him runs far too deep. I mustn't forget that it's the reason I was brought here. Having Matteo around, and being fucked seven days through to Sunday for the past few weeks has made it easy to forget what a complicated situation I'm in.

I eat a little of the food that was brought up for me but don't really feel hungry. Then, after showering and getting myself dressed, I decide to take advantage of Matteo's absence and explore the house.

I know the room I sleep in isn't his, he only occasionally spends the night sleeping beside me, so I wander the halls and check out the many rooms inside his mansion. I find one completely empty room, a storage closet, a gym and a massive bathroom before I twist the handle of the second, but last, door I have left to explore. When I step inside, what I see makes my breath catch in my throat. The room is spacious, like all the others, the walls crisp white and the carpet deep and soft under my bare feet. There's a cradle placed by the window and a rocking chair in the corner beside a bookshelf that is full of classic children's stories.

    I move toward the chair and sit in it, looking around the room and wondering how long it's been like this. The furniture looks antique, but the walls are freshly painted and the carpet smells new. I try to imagine myself sitting here with a child in my arms, and the vision comes so easily, I wonder if what Matteo so desperately wants to give me, is what I've always wanted. A chance to show love in a way that I never received it. I never knew my mother, she died a few days after I was born. I don't know what she looked like or how her voice sounded. She never sang me to sleep or hugged me in her arms when I got hurt or sick. My father tells me he loved her, but I have heard many rumors over the years that she was just his whore.

    I rest easy in the chair, rocking it back and forth while my hand rests on my flat stomach and I wonder what kind of mother I will make. Growing up the staff, my father paid to raise me, were firm but fair. They showed little affection toward me, yet still treated me like I was made of glass. I assume that was out of fear of my father. No one wanted to be responsible for the great Stevan Fucchini's little girl getting hurt. It's funny how people presume things, Matteo made the same presumption when he took me. He thought taking something precious to my father would weaken him, but there is a fault in his plan. The fact that the only thing my father holds precious is his empire. To him, I am just a possession, a pawn he can use in his game. Even the people I call friends were chosen for me by him, selected by their parents' stature, and what it can do for him. My father will be furious when he realizes Matteo has me, but not for the reasons Matteo assumes. He will be mad because something was taken from him, and no one takes from Stevan Fucchini.

    I don't know how long I sit rocking in the chair, but I feel a strong sense of comfort being in here, a hope for the future and the chance of a fresh start for me, and for Matteo. As I look out the huge window, I smile to myself as I imagine him chasing a toddler outside on his pristine lawn. And that's when I realize that I don't just want to please him. I want there to be a child growing inside me, just as much as he does.

CHAPTER SEVENTEEN

MATTEO

"Do you have work to do, today?" she asks, getting up from her seat at the breakfast table and sitting on the table in front of me. I can tell she's still mad at me for leaving without saying goodbye, but some things require urgency, and what I had to do couldn't be avoided.

"There is always work to do." I smile, taking her hand and licking the syrup from her fingers. "Did you have something in mind?"

"A walk around the gardens, maybe a drive into the local town. I don't even know where that is." Aria plays with the cuff of my shirt and tries being all cutesy, maybe her little act might work if I hadn't woken up with her lips wrapped around my cock. I swear the girl is developing some kind of syndrome, you hear about people falling in love with their captors as a coping mechanism. I don't want to be Aria's coping mechanism. I've learnt over the past few weeks that I want to be the start, and end, of her world.

"It is not safe for us to go into town, not while your father is looking for you," I tell her, lifting her nightdress up her body and leaning her back as I place soft delicate kisses over her flat, toned stomach to distract her from that fact. When I reach her tits I hold one in my hand as I roll my tongue around her nipple, and clasp it gently between my teeth.

"Ouch!" She winces, pulling away from me. I fight against her, forcing my body over hers, grabbing her wrists and pinning them to the table.

"You will take what I give you, and thank me for it." My tongue continues to circle her nipple, and I look up and watch her succumb to me. Her head falling back and her hips lifting higher to seek me out, rolling against my hard cock to create the friction she desires.

"I like you most when you're like this," I confess, slipping my nose over her cheek.

"Like what?" Aria's not stupid, she already knows the answer, but I'll give her it, regardless, because she likes the way it sounds.

"A needy, little cum-slut." I growl my words into her ear. "Look at you, so desperate, and fucking needy. I've trained you perfectly."

She proves me right when her hand slips between us and into the front of my slacks.

"You've never feared me the way you should, because this is what you wanted since you first saw me, even with your neck collared to the wall of my basement." I laugh at her cruelly as she works me through her fist.

"You won't hurt me," she whispers into my ear and when I pull back so I can look at her, she's wearing the most innocent look on her face.

To a normal man, hearing this would be a comfort, but not to me, it feels like a cruel twist, because she's right.

"You think you've got it all figured." I trace my fingers back down over her skin, pausing when I get to her stomach, and letting them linger.

LET VENGEANCE BE MINE

"You don't know the man that I am, or how dangerous I can be. No matter what happens between us, you should never forget that."

"Doesn't change anything. Like I said, you won't hurt me." She stares back at me defiantly.

I smile to give her a false sense of security, as I lift up one of her legs and place it over my shoulder, then taking the waist of her panties in both my hands, I fiercely tear the lace apart to grant me the access I need.

"Hurt...is what I do best." I push two of my fingers into her cunt, as far as I can get them, letting her juices coat them as I stroke the inside of her tight walls.

"I love how you're always so wet for me," I tell her, pulling them back out and sucking them before I trail her cum, mixed with my saliva, over the inside of the thigh I have lifted over my shoulder. When I force them back inside her, she lifts her hips from the table and groans.

"Did you miss me?" I ask, watching her work her needy, little pussy against me.

"Yes," she manages to answer, as I fuck her hard and fast with my fingers. She's still yet to show any sign of bleeding which I'm taking as a sign that all my hard work has paid off.

"I want your cock inside me," she begs, looking up at me with hungry eyes and determination.

"This cock?" I use my free hand to take it out and pump it through my fist, and Aria watches me, rubbing her lips together as she focuses.

"Look what I've turned you into." I smile at her proudly, as I work myself fast and hard. Her pussy clamps tight around my fingers as she imagines it inside her and when my pre-cum spills from the end of it, she sweeps it up with her finger and rubs her clit with it.

"You dirty, little whore." I hear the pride in my voice as I watch the innocent, little creature I stole, take what she needs, without shame or restraint.

"I'm not a whore." She shakes her head. "How can I be when it's only ever been you?" Her reminding me of that, has me withdrawing my fingers and flicking her hand away so I can push inside her. She moans deep as I fill her, clasping her nails into my forearm as I kiss the inside of her leg that's resting on my shoulder.

"You're so perfect. I'm so fucking proud of you." I tell her because I feel like she needs to hear it.

"Look at you, taking my cock so well, making it feel so fucking good for me."

She nods her head back at me, making my cock slide so easily in and out of her as her pussy becomes even wetter. "You're gonna come, aren't you?" I ask, already feeling myself getting close.

"Yes..."

"Wait for me, Aria. I'm almost there and we can come together." I thrust into her a little faster to speed it up, I can see how desperate she is, she won't last long and I'd hate to have to punish her.

"Okay, Princess, you can come now," I tell her when I'm almost ready. "Work the cum out of me too." I watch my cock slip in and out of her as her body turns rigid and her pussy tightens around me. "That's right, you want this cum so fucking bad, don't you?" She nods her head again, and when I see the tears in her eyes, I realize that she fucking means it. I drop her leg from my shoulder and wrap it around my waist, leaning over her body and kissing her lips as I fuck my cum as deep into her as I can get it. Then I hold still and watch as she takes it and the tears in her eyes start to spill.

"What's the matter?" I look at her curiously, not giving a fuck if she sees my weakness when I cradle her face and wipe them away with my thumb. "Nothing." She shakes her head, being defiant.

"Aria, if you don't tell me what's wrong I can't fix it." I don't like the helplessness of how that feels.

"I think I've fallen in love with you," she confesses, looking up at me with big, innocent tear-filled eyes. I should make her take her words back, I should want to punish her for them because none of this was part of the plan. But I don't. I kiss her gratefully instead, holding her tighter to my body, and keeping my cock buried deep inside her, feeling like the luckiest man on the fucking planet.

CHAPTER EIGHTEEN

ARIA

"You look pretty today." Matteo stares at me as he does up the cuffs of his shirt. It's amazing what a compliment from him can do. It puts an instant smile on my face and makes my stomach flip, especially when he sits on the mattress next to where I'm laid and rests his hand on the other side of my body.

"Your period is due," he whispers, leaning over my body, so his breath tickles my ear.

"How do you...?" I give up asking. I would say I'm surprised but nothing about this man shocks me, anymore.

"I have an app on my phone." Matteo kisses my cheek before standing back up and lifting his suit jacket from the end of the bed.

"You shouldn't get your hopes up. Women are late on their periods all the time. I've never really kept track of mine." I shrug, starting to feel a little pressured. I know how disappointed Matteo was last month when I came on my period, he didn't speak, touch or look at me for five days. I don't know how I'll cope if he does that to me, again. Which is a sure sign that I'm in serious need of therapy.

"What's that look for?" Matteo watches me through the

reflection of the mirror, as he straightens up his jacket and checks himself over.

"I'm just thinking about what happened last month. You put me back in the basement." I wait for his reaction. Something tells me no one has ever made Matteo Romano face up to his behavior, before.

He looks pissed, and I can't figure out if it's at me or at himself.

"Come here." He turns around and summons me to him with his finger. His eyes drop to the spot on the floor where he wants me, and like a desperate little moth to the flame, I climb out of bed and go to him.

"That's not going to happen again." He has a deadly, serious look on his face, one that makes me believe him.

"Is that your version of an apology?" I smile, taking the lapels of his jacket in both my hands. It's unhealthy for me to miss him before he's even gone. But I do. If I had my way he would never leave.

"No, it's reassurance. I never apologize." He keeps that serious look on his face and when I slide my hands up his chest and wrap them around his neck, he lowers his head so his forehead presses into mine.

"I'll pick us up a test while I'm out," he whispers.

"Maybe, we should wait a few days. Like I said, it's normal to be a little late."

"Patience isn't my strong point." He places a kiss on my lips before pulling away.

"Where are you going, today?" I ask as he makes his way toward the door.

"I have business to take care of," The smile he gives me confirms he isn't going to give me any more information than that.

"And what time will you be home?" I check, following him to the door and placing my hand over his.

"Needy today, aren't we?" He has a smug smirk on his face that suggests he likes it and, as attractive as it is, it makes me want to punch him.

"I just get lonely when you're not around," I admit, avoiding eye contact and feeling ridiculous.

"It won't be like this, forever." He lifts my chin with the crook of his finger and almost looks like he feels sorry for me. I feel sorry for me too, especially when I realize that I've forgotten how it is to be outside of his fortress. For almost two months the only people I have seen are Matteo and his guards.

"You know I would never run from you, don't you?" I assure him, meaning every word. Whatever this is, no matter how fucked-up it is, I would never want my life to go back to how it was.

"Doesn't mean I'm prepared to risk it." Matteo kisses my forehead before he leaves.

∽

I went back to bed and took a nap after Matteo left. When I wake up and look at the time, I'm surprised to see that it's already past noon. Lately, I've been feeling exhausted. I've put it down to the fact Matteo can't go a few hours without being inside me, but this is a different level of tiredness. One that could have me going back to sleep again, if I let myself. I get out of bed and head for the shower so I can freshen myself up. And when I flick through the wardrobe of clothes, that Matteo has supplied me with over the past few weeks, I pick out something comfortable and head into the kitchen to find myself something to eat. The house seems empty, even the housekeeper, who is always kind to me, doesn't seem to be around. As soon as I open the refrigerator, the smell inside it makes me turn up my nose. There's nothing in here that's off, from what I can see, but there's also nothing I could stomach eating. Closing the door, I take an orange from the fruit bowl instead. I'm heading into the living room, to see what's on T.V., when my feet stop in their tracks and I find myself staring at the middle-aged woman who's standing in the hall. She's well presented, with eyes I recognize, and long, dark-black hair that she has pinned up neatly in a French pleat.

"Hello." She looks just as surprised to see me as I am her, and as she steps forward her eyes scan me cautiously.

"Hey." I tug at the sweater I'm wearing, feeling nervous and a little overwhelmed by her presence.

"And, you are?" She widens her eyes, expecting an answer.

"Aria," I answer her before I have a chance to think about whether I'm supposed to or not.

"Aria." She repeats my name and nods her head as if she approves, "And do you know where my son is, Aria?"

"Matteo?" Strange as it sounds, I never took into consideration the fact he would have a mother.

"Yes. Matteo." She stares at me, impatiently.

"He...um. He left earlier this morning. I don't know when he will be back. I don't think he was expecting you." I smile nervously.

"A mother never has to be invited." She takes off her jacket and shoves it at me before striding through to the living room. I quickly hang it on the cloak rack by the door and follow after her, unsure if that's what she expects of me, or not.

"So, are you one of his whores?" She takes a cigarette from a silver case, placing it between her red-painted lips, and I try not to get distracted by her presence while I come up with an answer for her.

"No, I'm um…" I have no idea what to say because I don't know what I am to Matteo. Just that, he's everything to me.

"Sit." She taps the seat beside her, and I react the same way I do whenever her son gives me an order…obediently.

She lights her cigarette with a Zippo and shocks the breath out of me when she clasps her talons around my chin and moves my face, to examine it.

"You're pretty. And young. Too young for him," she laughs.

"Nineteen," I confirm defensively, shifting uncomfortably when she releases me.

"And where did he find you?" She tokes back on her cigarette.

"Mrs Romano." Demitri comes to my rescue when he steps through the door and, for the first time since I've been here, I see a little fear on his face.

"Ahhh, Demitri, perhaps you can shine some light on my son's whereabouts?" She raises her perfectly-maintained eyebrows at him, and I watch him shake his head as the words get tangled in his mouth.

"He will be back soon. Perhaps, you will be more comfortable waiting for him in his office? I could fix you a drink."

"I am quite comfortable sitting here with Anna, we will both take a Martini and make it dirty." She winks at him before turning back around to face me, and he offers me a helpless look as he heads off to get her what she wants.

"The boy's father was a friend of my husband's, it's why Matteo keeps him around," She rolls her eyes at me before she drags on her cigarette, again.

"You were telling me how you met my son." She gets right back to where we left off, and I feel my chest tighten with anxiety as I try to come up with an answer.

"At a party." I swallow thickly, knowing what a terrible liar I am.

"Matteo rarely goes to parties, whose party was it?" She looks as though she's trying to catch me in a lie, and it's working.

"I can't recall, I was a little wasted. Me and my friends ended up there, I met Matteo and the rest is… history," I laugh awkwardly, grateful when Anita, the housekeeper, comes through with a tray. She nods her head at Matteo's mother before placing two paper napkins on the table, along with the dirty Martinis she ordered, and I immediately reach for mine and take a sip.

It tastes a little fuzzy on my tongue, and when I swallow I feel a wave of nausea that I didn't expect.

"Are you ok, dear?" Mrs Romano asks, doing a good job of acting like she's concerned.

"I'm just not used to drinking," I admit, stirring the olive around the glass and trying not to throw up.

"Oh, I thought you said you were 'wasted' the night you met my son?" She has a victorious look on her face and all I can do is offer her another awkward smile.

"Mother." Matteo's voice has us both standing on our feet, and when he walks through the door his eyes immediately go to the glass in my hand and narrow furiously.

"Darling, how are you?" Mrs Romano heads towards him with outstretched arms and, as she embraces him, he gives me a cold look over her shoulder.

"Demitri called and said you were here. I wasn't expecting you." His voice remains stern despite the affection she shows him.

"So, it seems," She looks at me back toward me and smirks.

It's now that I notice how different Matteo looks from when he left. His hair is flopped onto his forehead, he's not wearing his jacket, and the cuffs of his shirt are rolled up to his elbows.

"Is there something you wanted?" He heads towards me and takes the drink from my hand, sniffing it then shaking his head before he places it back on the table.

"Just to see that you are okay. It's been a while, darling." His mother smiles at him sweetly as his hand slides around my hip and his fingers dig discreetly into my flesh.

"I'm very well. Excellent, in fact." Matteo almost seems a little nervous, himself, and despite knowing I'm in trouble, I find that quite amusing.

"Anna, here, tells me the two of you met at a party. It has been a while since you socialized. I'm happy to hear that you are feeling better." There's a bite of sarcasm in her tone, "Perhaps, now that you are feeling sociable again, we will see you at Gerald and Colotta's engagement party? Anna, too, of course." She looks between us.

"Maybe." Matteo shrugs. "And her name is Aria," he corrects her.

"My apologies." Her smile tells me the apology she makes is fake but I nod to accept it, anyway.

"Matteo, I have something private I wish to discuss with you."

"Of course. Head into my office. I'll be right there," he tells her, and after she picks up her glass from the table, she presses a tight kiss on each of my cheeks before she walks back out to the hall.

"What the *fuck* are you doing?" Matteo barely gives her a chance to leave before he spins me around.

"Entertaining your mother, by all accounts." I hit back, he has no right to be mad at me, not after what I've just had to endure.

"I didn't mean that. I mean *that*." He points to the glass on the table. "A little reckless, considering what condition you might be in, don't you think?" He raises his eyebrows at me.

"She ordered them, I couldn't exactly tell her that I might be carrying your child, could I? Matteo, that was hell. I had no idea what to tell her."

"I'll deal with her, In the meantime, you go upstairs and wait for me in your room," he orders, still looking mad as he marches off toward his office. I want to chase after him and slap him for treating me like a child, but the thought of being faced with that woman again has me, huffing in frustration and taking myself back upstairs.

CHAPTER NINETEEN

MATTEO

I find Aria in her room, sitting in the chair that's placed in the corner, with her arms folded and a scowl on her face. She looks pretty when she's angry, and that makes me want to punish her even more.

"Come." I go straight to her, taking her hand and dragging her up on her feet. Then, leading her into the bathroom, I take the pregnancy testing kit from my back pocket and start opening the box.

I can see the confused way she's looking at me from the corner of my eye when I neatly unfold the instruction leaflet and lay them out on the basin unit.

"You want to do that, now?" She doesn't look angry anymore. She looks nervous instead.

"Yes," I answer, taking the plastic stick in my hand and removing the cap from the part she has to pee on. My eyes gesture to the toilet and she makes that sarcastic, little laugh that sends me fucking crazy.

"While you're in the room?" Her eyes stretch in disbelief when she realizes I'm not going anywhere.

"Matteo, I'm not gonna pee in front of you."

I remain silent, stepping toward her so my body presses against hers and forces her to start walking backwards.

"This is ridiculous." She shakes her head, making a laugh that sounds much more nervous, now. Then a shocked gasp echoes around the room when I grip the waist of her yoga pants and drag them down to her knees.

"Sit." I glance over her shoulder at the toilet that's directly behind her, and despite the defiance on her face, she does exactly as she's told.

"I'm not going to be able to do it with you watching me like that." She snatches the stick from my hand, and I nod my head curtly before I turn my back, to give her her privacy, and cross my arms while I wait.

"Make sure you get it on the absorbent—"

"I figured that!" she snaps. And it doesn't matter how furious I am about what I saw downstairs, I can't help smirking to myself.

"There, done." The sound of the flush has me turning back around, where she presents me with the stick and a sarcastic smile. I take it from her and place it on the basin unit along with the instructions.

"Now, what?" she asks, reaching on her toes to try and look over my shoulder at the result. The test takes three minutes, according to the instructions and I can think of a good way to pass the time.

"Now, we talk about the fact you were drinking." I frown.

"I told you what happened. Your mom ordered the drinks. I was getting worked up by all her questions and so, I took a sip." She reacts to my silence by continuing her rant. "It tasted vile, I wasn't going to drink anymore. I wasn't thinking…I mean we don't even know if I'm pregnant, yet. I'm not even a day late." She makes another not-so-sly attempt to look past me at the result.

"It was a careless thing to do. I should take you over my knee and make your ass flush, for it."

"Well, are you going to?" The sassy, little smile she makes implies that she likes the sound of it.

"Depends on what the result of this test is." I clench my jaw. I've been feeling nervous all morning, way more nervous than I expected to be.

"I'm scared too." She reaches out to take my hand like she can read my mind, and I let my defenses slip, squeezing her fingers between mine as I grip it.

"Has it been three minutes, yet?" she asks.

"It hasn't even been one." I check my watch. Time is passing so slowly, I swear I can hear it ticking.

"What did your mother want?" Aria asks, attempting to make it pass quicker.

"I don't want to talk about that, now." I swallow the lump in my throat and close my eyes.

"Matteo." She steps a little closer, her free hand sliding up my shirt and resting on my jaw. "I want you to promise me that, no matter what, you'll make sure we stay together." I open my eyes and crease my brow at her.

"Sure, I'm scared, but I know that if I have you, everything will be ok. If that test is positive and we're starting a family together, I need you to know I'm all in." She drops her hand to her stomach and makes me forget that I'm mad with her. My hand reaches around her, cupping the back of her dainty neck and dragging her close so I can kiss her lips.

The reason I brought her here doesn't seem important anymore. I don't want revenge, I want everything she just said. I want a family.

I hold her close, breathing her in and waiting for the minutes to pass.

"I think it'll be ready now," she whispers, looking up at me with a smile that I think I'd die for. And suddenly, I feel like I don't deserve any of this. This girl in front of me, may have been born into this world, but she's innocent to it.

"Matteo, it's time to check." She bites her lip like she's excited and I don't know when this became a thing she wanted, I don't understand how, but I feel a flutter in my chest when I nod my head and let her step past me. She steps up to the basin unit and picks up the stick, when she spins back around, the huge smile on her face gives me the answer I need.

"We did it!" She holds the stick out as evidence and when I see the two pink lines in the window, I quickly move closer and check it against the instructions. I don't know why it comes as such a shock. This is what I've been planning. I've lost count of the amount of times I've come inside her to make sure of it; but holding that stick in my hand, confirming it, makes everything suddenly seem very fucking real.

"Matteo, are you gonna say something?" She giggles like this is something she's been wanting her whole life. Not something that she was stolen for and had forced upon her.

"Matteo, we're going to have a baby." She takes my face in her hands and forces me to look at her. "We actually *did it*." I'm hearing every word she's saying, but finding it hard to believe it's true.

"Come with me." I take her hand in mine and drag her out the bathroom, through the bedroom and into the corridor. My guard stands a little taller as we pass him and when I get to my bedroom door, she stares at me in confusion when I open it.

"Is this your room?" she asks, looking around her at the tall ceiling and the dark walls.

"It's *our* room." I grab her and lift her onto my body, carrying her to my bed and laying her out on the mattress. All of a sudden she looks so different. Even more precious and vulnerable. My instinct to protect her has just multiplied by a fucking hundred.

"You want me to sleep in here, from now on?" She sits up on her elbows and watches me lift up her sweater. Of course, her stomach is still flat and tightly toned, but knowing that she now carries my child inside it, makes me want to kiss it all over.

"What are you doing?" She giggles as I press my lips all over her skin. I can't remember a time when I've felt as happy as I do, right now, and I refuse to let any paranoia of someone taking them away from me ruin this moment.

I kiss my way up her body until I get to her lips and then I kiss her there too.

"Are you feeling happy, Matteo Romano?" she asks with a clever smile on her lips. She's proud to be pregnant with my child inside her, I can tell by the glint in her eyes.

"I'm feeling on top of the goddamn world" I admit.

CHAPTER TWENTY

MATTEO

TWO MONTHS LATER

"Why are you so tense? Today's supposed to be exciting." Aria swallows the last of her pancake from the fork, I'm holding to her mouth. I have to be really strict with her at meal times, if she had her way she wouldn't eat, at all. Since she's been pregnant, the baby's only been making her feel sick, luckily she keeps whatever I can get into her, down.

"I *am* excited." I stroke my hand across her tummy, there's still no sign of her condition from the outside, but it won't be long before she starts to show.

"Are you scared there might be something wrong? I've done everything your doctor friend told me to. I've eaten the right food, taken that folic, whatever, tablet. Apart from the nausea, I feel great." She tries to reassure me, but that's not why I'm anxious about today.

I have kept Aria in my protective bubble for the past four months. Today we are having to step out of it, and that concerns me.

"Not at all, our child's going to be perfect." I put her mind at rest, kissing her cheek before I gently shift her off my lap and get up from the table. "I just have a few things to take care of and then we can leave." I fake her a smile and head for my office, sucking air through my nostrils and trying to remain calm. Demitri must pick up on my mood because he follows after me, efficiently.

"Okay, out with it. What's wrong?" he asks, closing the door behind him.

"What's fuckin' wrong?" I stare back at him, wondering if he really is that stupid. "Are you forgetting what happened the last time I took a girl to a sonogram appointment?" My hand slides through my hair as I blow out a frustrated breath.

"Matteo, that is not gonna happen again. The car has been checked, rechecked and triple-checked, and I will personally stay with it the whole time."

"It's not just that. Her being out there is a risk, what if she's seen? What if…?" I stop myself because saying the words out loud will remind me of how wrong they are.

"Matteo." Demitri gives me that look that reminds me nothing I say will faze him.

"What if a glimpse back into reality makes her realize how fucked-up all this is?" I say the words that have been going round and round in my head for weeks now.

"Matteo, my friend…" Demitri shakes his head and laughs at me. "…I don't know how you did it, but that girl is in love with you. I don't think there is anything that can change that."

"There are plenty of things that could change that," I point out, tensing my fists in frustration. "Her feelings for me are delusional. I'm not the man she thinks I am."

"You *are* that man for her." He shrugs, taking a seat on the opposite side of my desk. "I've known you for twenty-five years and that girl has brought out a side of you I don't recognise. I don't need to tell you that she's changed you. This plan of yours has gone far beyond vengeance. You're in lo–"

"Stop right there." I cut him off. "I care for Aria, deeply. She fascinates me, in a way I don't understand, but I do *not* love her. You and I both know I am incapable of that." I make that point very clear.

"Okay, but just to let you know...That girl, you don't love, is really excited to see that baby, you knocked her up with, today. Fabier has closed his practice for the morning and I will have two other cars with guards in to escort you there. *Nothing* is going to go wrong." He wears a clever smirk as he gets up from his chair, and after he's headed out the door, I rest both my palms flat on my desk and take some steady breaths.

It's a few minutes later when the door creaks open and Aria steps inside.

"You ready?" She smiles at me, confirming that Demetri's right, she is really excited about today, and I won't let my anxieties ruin it for her.

"Yeah, I'm ready." I pull myself together and go to her.

"Let's go meet our baby." The smile on her face is so genuine it reminds me, again, that I don't deserve it, and as I take her hand in mine and lead her out to the car, I wonder how far I'd go to keep it there.

∼

Fabier has stuck to his word, his practice is empty when we arrive. He doesn't even have another member of staff here. Then again, I had no reason to doubt him, not for the amount of money I'm paying to get him out of the shit, he's in.

Aria lies on the bed beside the screen, while we wait for

him to come back with her blood results from last week. She's looking a lot more nervous, now we're here; the way she keeps flattening out the tissue paper, she has tucked into the top of her jeans, proves that.

"It feels really real being here doesn't it?" She tries to make conversation while her eyes wander around the room.

"Yeah, it does." I smile back at her, thinking of all the things that could go wrong, while we're here.

"Are you nervous—?"

The door, opening, interrupts us before I can answer and when Fabier walks in he smiles at us both before sitting on the stool, in front of the sonogram machine.

"You'll be pleased to know all the blood work, I took from you last week, has come back normal," he assures us, and I nod my head feeling relieved. I made sure every test available was carried out in case there was any extra care Aria needed. She's been so tired lately, and although Fabier said that is normal in the early stages of pregnancy, I have been worried about her.

"All that leaves for us to do, now, is have a look and see how things are developing." He smiles as he picks up his instrument and covers it in a clear gel. Aria reaches for my hand, squeezing it tight as she looks up and the ceiling and takes a breath.

I watch the screen, intently, as he moves the thing over her stomach, and when the image on the screen becomes clear, I clench her hand a little tighter.

"There we are." Fabier gestures his eyes at the screen and when Aria eventually turns her head to look for herself, her eyes fill up with tears.

"That's our baby?" she checks as if she doesn't quite believe it.

"It sure is, and this…" Fabier presses something on his computer and the sound of galloping horses fills the room. "…is your baby's heartbeat."

Aria makes a cute, relieved laugh as she stares at the screen and listens. And Fabier explains that he has to take some measurements while she remains transfixed.

"This all estimates that you're around 11 weeks and 2 days along," he confirms, once he's done. Then placing the instrument back in its holder, he leaves the image of our child on the screen and gives Aria more tissue to clean herself up.

"So, what now?" I ask, rising to my feet and watching him move over to the printer, on the other side of the room.

"Now, we wait. The mother is healthy, your baby is developing as it should. We will do some follow-up appointments in the coming weeks but I can come to your home for those. I know you prefer it that way." He clears his throat as he hands over the images that just came out of the printer.

I look down at the picture in my hand. All this feels so much different to the way it did before. I know the pain of loss now, and the pressure to keep them both safe is overwhelming.

"And what about the sex?" Aria swings her legs over the side of the bed and goes to stand up.

"I can tell you the gender if you wish, the tests you had carried out determined it." Fabier moves back over to the file.

"Not that kind of sex. I mean, physical sex." Her cheeks flush pink. "I've tried telling Matteo it's safe but he is insistent that it's not." I watch her chew on her thumbnail, awkwardly, and shake my head at her. Ever since I saw those two pink lines my sole intention has been to make sure everything goes well. I don't want to lose another child. Maybe, I'm being over-cautious, and if she thinks for a second that I haven't suffered from it, she's wrong. But I will do whatever it takes to ensure this pregnancy goes well.

"It is only recommended that you abstain if the pregnancy is high risk. Like I said, this one is completely normal," Fabier assures her, and the victorious, little smile she makes, as she hops off the bed, makes my cock hard.

"You heard it for yourself," she tells me, as she steps closer.

"Wait...did you say you knew the sex of the baby?" I check I heard him right, something needs to distract me from the fact I just got the doctor's go-ahead to give in to Aria's demands, after two months of restraining.

"Yes, would you like to know?" He holds the file in his hand.

"Yes, I do," I answer back immediately. It's not something Aria or I have discussed but suddenly I feel like I have to know.

"You're having a son." He smiles as he walks past us and out the door, and my mouth drops in shock as I look from him and then to Aria.

"Did you hear that?" I shake my head in disbelief. "I'm having a son. You're giving me a fucking son." I can't describe the feeling I get as I repeat those words, it's something that goes beyond happiness and fulfillment, and it has me lifting Aria off her feet and backing her up onto that bed she was just laid on.

"What are you doing?" The way she whispers and giggles at the same time is fucking adorable and encourages the thought that's already planted in my head.

"You heard what he just said. I've held off on you for long enough." I unbuckle my belt and release my cock, sliding it through my fist while Aria looks around the room in shock. Then, with a daring look in her eyes, she quickly shimmies her jeans and panties off her hips.

"I did tell you everything would be okay." She opens her legs, and grips at my shirt, tugging me closer. She hasn't made abstaining from sex easy on me, and now I'm wondering how the fuck I've lain beside this woman for two whole months, without being inside her. I deserve a fucking medal!

She rests back on the bed, looking up at me like a temptress, and I take her narrow hips in my hands and hold her while my cock brushes between her pussy lips. She's soaking, fucking wet but then, just lately, she always is. She's had to make do with coming from external stimulation alone, and now I know everything's okay and the doc's given us the all-clear, she's about to be reminded how it feels to be full of me.

"This is gonna have to be quick, but when we get back home, I'm going to make up for all the time I've held back on you," I assure her, watching her eyes widen and her lips raise into a seductive smile when I push inside her. I can't bring myself to fuck her hard and fast the way I want to. She feels far too precious now, and as I let both my thumbs stroke over her lower stomach, where I know our son is growing healthily, I feel a real sense of pride.

"I've missed this," Aria whispers, looking between us and watching as my cock moves in and out of her, soft and steadily.

"A son," I repeat the words the doctor said, looking down at her flat stomach in complete awe, and still not believing it. When she starts to move her hips a little more desperately against mine, the intensity of how long it's been since we had this, starts to take its toll. The way her pussy tightens around me, and the fact she announces she's going to come, has me thrusting one last time, tipping back my head and releasing deep inside her. It's been so long since I've come like this, that my legs shake and I have to steady myself on the edge of the bed.

"I can't believe you just fucked me in the doctor's office." Aria laughs and when I look back down at her, I try to remember seeing a sight more beautiful. "He could have walked back in here, anytime."

"Would you have cared?" I ask, picking her jeans up off the floor and helping her get back into them.

"I don't think I would have." She wets her lips with her tongue before she grabs at my tie and kisses me.

"Come on, let's get out here. I have plans for us." I tell her, desperate to get her back to the safety of our home.

CHAPTER TWENTY-ONE

ARIA

ONE MONTH LATER

"Do you think she's going to notice?" I study my figure in the mirror. Over the past few weeks, my stomach has become noticeably rounder, and it now sticks out over the waistline of my panties.

"I don't care if she does." Matteo steps up beside me, placing his hand over my tiny bump. He can't seem to get enough of it, which I guess is a good thing since I'm only going to get bigger. Since seeing our baby on the screen for real, Matteo has barely left my side. I've come to learn a lot more about him, and the more of this side I see of him, the easier it becomes to forget how I got here.

"Are you sure this is a good idea?" I look up at him warily, the last time I met Matteo's mother I was a nervous wreck. Her coming here for lunch, today, isn't something I've been looking forward to.

"Now's as good a time as any, to tell her she's going to be a grandma." He shrugs.

"Wait, you're going to tell her about this?" I stare back at him in shock.

"Well, it's not exactly the kind of thing we can keep secret for long." He laughs as he moves to the dresser and picks up the necklace he bought for me last week.

"I don't think she's going to approve. She doesn't like me, I could tell from–"

"What have I told you about getting worked up? It's not good for our son." Once he's fastened the diamonds around my neck, he pats his hand over my tummy and smiles.

"Well, how about you don't invite your mother over for awkward lunches and then I won't have to?" I look back at him through the mirror and give him a smart-assed smile.

"Don't look at me like that, you know what you behaving like a brat does to me." He spins me around and tugs my bottom lip between his teeth. The idea of him being rough makes my pussy leak into my panties, but I know this is as rough as I'm going to get it until I'm done being pregnant. Matteo only takes me gently, these days, I miss the way he used to pin me to a wall or slap my ass while he fucked me. And I know, from the tension in his body, that he misses it too.

"I'm just nervous," I admit, playing with the lapel of his jacket and giving him the cutesy eyes that, just recently, I've learnt will always get me my way.

"We'll get this over with and then I'll make it up to you." He moves away from me so he can fasten his cuffs.

"Well, since we're telling your mom about the baby, don't you think we should tell my father?" I step over to the wardrobe and take out the pretty, baby blue, summer dress that's hanging up. Matteo looks far too formal for lunch on the lawn and has stomped all over my idea to wear jeans and a tee.

"Tell your father?" He almost chokes on his laugh.

"Yes, Matteo. My father. Our son's grandfather. Like you

said, this isn't something we can hide forever. How long do you expect him to buy my story about rebelling and traveling the world? Do you plan on keeping me and our baby locked up in this house, forever?" I can see what I'm saying pisses him off, but I stand firm and wait for his answer.

"And what, do you suppose, I tell him? That I hate him so much, I took his daughter and forced my child inside her?"

"It wasn't like that, and you know it." I look away from him when I get a reminder of how fucked-up all this would sound to an outsider. "Besides, I have an idea on how we could make our situation more acceptable." I slide the dress over my head and wait for him to come over and zip up the back.

Matteo carefully steps around me, lifting the zip up over my body, antagonizing slowly. Then leaning over my shoulder he whispers into my ear, so softly, that it tickles.

"Let's hear it then, Princess." His hands curl around my waist and he tugs me back against his body.

"I think we should face up to this." I spin myself around so I'm looking right at him. "We tell him that we met at a party, just like I did your mom. We tell him that we're having a baby together." I take Matteo's hand and rest it over my stomach, "And the two of you find a way to settle your differences for the sake of this little boy we're going to have."

"That's not going to happen, Aria." Matteo shakes his head, and I wish I could read the expression on his face.

"You seem to forget that, for my whole life, my father has wanted to use me for his advantage, an alliance with you would be an advantage."

"Your father hated my father, he hates me, and I'm pretty certain he will hate our son." Matteo gives it to me unfiltered and I can't pretend his words don't hurt.

"Will you ever tell me what he did to you?" I ask, brushing

my thumb over his stubbly jaw when I see the pain and anger in his eyes that was there when I first met him.

"Come on, Mother doesn't like to be kept waiting." He smiles at me, sadly, before moving toward the door and when he holds it open for me, I take a deep breath and move out.

"Darling." Mrs Romano greets her son with a hug, before offering me a tight smile. "You're still here, I see." She raises her eyebrows, unimpressively, as she takes a seat at the table that's been positioned to look out over the mountains.

"She'll be here indefinitely," Matteo assures her, wrapping his hand around my thigh under the table, like he's afraid I'll bolt. The sarcastic look she gives me is savage and I lower myself by throwing one back at her.

"So, what was it that was so important that you dragged me away from Malibu?" She lifts her cigarette case off the table and takes one out, placing it between her lips, and when she goes to reach for her lighter, Matteo slams his hand over hers.

"I'm going to have to ask you not to do that," he tells her firmly, and the look she gives him back appears to be as confused, as it is unimpressed.

"It's not good for the baby," Matteo adds, with a straight look on his face as he breaks the news. My stomach flips like I'm going to be sick when her eyes move from his, down to where his hand now rests, protectively, over my stomach.

"Baby?" She swallows uncomfortably, then tries to remain calm as she carefully places the cigarette back in her case and snaps it shut.

"Yes, we are expecting a son. Aria is 16 weeks along, now." I hear both pride and determination in Matteo's voice, and while his mother's eyelashes blink a little more rapidly, I feel the tension in his fingers become tighter.

"I could get you the picture if you want to see it. We had a sonogram a few weeks ago." I try to cut through the frosty atmosphere, and she shakes her head back at me, still too stunned to speak.

"What a convenient mistake to make." She eventually manages to say something, taking the bottle of wine from the bucket on the table and holding up her hand at the server, who attempts to take over, so she can fill her glass almost to the brim.

"Quite the opposite. The child was planned," Matteo informs her unapologetically, and she laughs, in tiny, little bursts that soon become hysterical.

"She's Stevan Fucchini's fucking *daughter,* Matteo!" Her head shakes back at him like she's sure he's lost the plot. "But you knew that, didn't you? If you think this is going to reunite two families that have been at war for decades, you are very wrong...Did recent events not teach you anything?" She knocks back half of the wine in her glass and takes out a little trinket box from her purse. One that she opens up and dabs her finger into the white powder inside, before snorting up her nostril.

"Mother, is that really necessary? We're at the lunch table for Christ's sake!"

"I think it's *very* fucking necessary, you have just informed me that you have knocked up the daughter of your father's biggest enemy. Excuse me for needing to take the edge off." I feel like a spare part sitting here and listening to them both. But as much as I want to get up and run away, I fear my legs wouldn't carry me.

"My original intentions were not for resolution, but things have changed." Matteo's words give me hope and make tears slowly creep into my eyes. That happens a lot, lately. I put it down to pregnancy hormones. I cried watching a mama bird feed her chick when I was reading on the balcony yesterday.

"What would your father say, if he was here?" Matteo's mother shakes her head at him in disgust.

"I care as much about that as I do your opinion. I asked you here, today, so I could inform you of our *happy* news. You can either celebrate it with us or get the fuck out of my house." The look he gives her is cold and I'm surprised when she holds his stare and picks up her wine glass.

"To the next Romano heir," she says, sarcastically, before lifting her glass and finishing what's left in it.

CHAPTER TWENTY-TWO

MATTEO

"Today must have been tough for you." I pull back the covers when Aria starts walking toward the bed. She's wearing just her panties and seeing that tiny bump of hers sticking over the waistline of them has my cock steel, fucking, hard.

"It was awful." She slides in beside me, snuggling into my chest and looking up at me through her lashes.

"Talking about varicose veins and piles over a Caesar salad was *not* my idea of a fun afternoon. I swear she managed to cram every pregnancy horror story, she's ever heard, into that hour," she points out, but soon eases up when I slide my hand into the front of her panties and start rubbing my finger against her clit, she mewls like a satisfied, little kitten. I love the way she gets turned on so easily, and when I start to slowly tease her entrance, she grabs my wrist to hold it steady.

"I won't let you distract me from the conversation we need to have." She moves quickly, shifting her body so it's straddling mine.

"Now, who's distracting who?" I look up at her and snigger, taking one of her perfect, round tits in my palm and squeezing.

I know how sensitive they are, and that it will bring her a little pain, but it's the kind she needs, and when I feel her thighs gently clutch around my hips, it only confirms I'm right.

"Did you mean what you said at the table, about your intentions changing? Do you think you could do that for me?" She scrutinises me with her eyes like she's trying to read all the thoughts in my head.

"Honestly?" I don't know what to say to her, I don't have the answers myself. "I don't know. I have no idea where to go from here." My fingertips trail down her skin and rest over my stomach. "All that matters is this, and keeping you both safe."

Aria's hand flattens over mine to keep it there. She's really proud of the fact she's starting to show, and I've caught her admiring her new figure in the mirror, more often than once, these past few days.

"I get that. But we will have to face reality, soon. If my dad saw this side of you–"

"No one sees this side of me, Aria, even *I* don't know this fucking side of me. It scares me." I hate admitting that to her, but something about this beautiful, young woman seems to drain the truth out of me.

"I can't be weak, a lot of people rely on the decisions I make. I'm used to that, I bear the weight of it. But having you depend on those decisions feels like…" I can't find the words to describe it, other than soul-crushing.

"You will make the right choices, for all of us." She smiles back at me so sweetly, that I feel it crush even more.

I slide my hand up her body, moving through the valley between her tits before gently taking her throat. It's been a while since I handled her roughly, I won't take the risk, but I know how much she misses it. She's always begging for me to fuck her harder when I'm inside her, and the spark of thrill I see in her eyes when I tense my fingers a little, tells me just how much.

"Just give me a little more time to think it over." My voice comes out weak, almost like I'm begging her, and when I drag her body down onto mine and kiss her lips, she fidgets her hips to try and get some friction from the rock-hard cock I've got resting between her legs.

"You need me to take care of that?" I ask, hooking the finger from my free hand into the side of her panties, and clearing a path so my cock can brush against her sensitive flesh. She makes that noise again, the one that tells me we won't have to speak about her father again, tonight.

∼

After Aria falls asleep, I head straight to the room where I keep all my gym equipment and turn the speed on the treadmill right up. I used to take a jog in the forest that surrounds my home, every day. But, these days, I won't be away from Aria unless it's absolutely necessary. I can't get Fucchini out of my head. I could never predict how he would react if he found out, and I have no idea how I would respond to being face-to-face with the man who killed an innocent woman, and my child. My feet thud hard against the belt and I feel the sweat pour from my skin. It's not till my lungs feel like they'll collapse that I hit the cool-down mode and allow myself to catch my breath.

"It's late." Demitri's voice comes from behind me, and when I glance back at him over my shoulder, I wonder how long he's been there.

"Did my mother get home, okay?" I check, knowing it will have been a draining task for him to have to drive her all the way back to Malibu.

"She's insufferable," he tells me, dumping a brown case file on the weight bench beside me.

"What's that?" I step off the treadmill, grabbing the hand towel that's resting over the bar and draping it over the back of my neck

"That's the file, I had hacked, from the computer of the private investigator Fucchini has hired to find his daughter. Your name is on a list of suspects that could have potentially kidnapped her," he informs me.

"That's shit. Aria spoke to her dad a few days ago. He still thinks she's *finding* herself," I assure him, not even bothering to open the file.

"Clearly fuckin' not, Matteo. It's all there, in black and white. You know what a clever man Fucchini is, did you honestly expect him to believe her story?"

"You forget who you are talking to." I square up to him, his new information has put a bitter taste in my mouth. His attitude, and how he's delivering it, is making me want to throttle him.

"I don't know *who* I'm talking to anymore, Matteo. You're detached, nothing matters to you but that damn girl. Did you know we had a whole shipment disappear last week? 150k worth of cocaine just vanished. And do you know who dealt with that? Me.

And all while you were upstairs flicking through the big *fucking* book of baby names, deciding what to name your son. A son who will have nothing to inherit, if his father doesn't wake up and start living in the real fucking world."

I act on instinct, balling up my fist and throwing it at his face.

I love Demitri like a brother but I will not tolerate his disrespect.

He takes my punch well, using his thumb to wipe away the blood that drips from his lip.

"What happened to the shipment?" I ask, once I've found my calm, again.

"Some biker gang, who Phillippe thought he could trust, double-crossed him."

"And where is it now?" I catch my breath while I wait for his answer.

"Back where it belongs," he answers me, sharply.

"And the bikers?"

"Dealt with, I had their clubhouse burned down and each one of them killed," he informs me.

"Thank you," I speak humbly when I realize he's right. I have been off the ball, lately. It must have been a lot of pressure for him.

"I get you're stressed, Matteo. I'm your best friend. I'm here for you and that's never going to change. But you should take a look at that file. If you want to keep that girl and the baby she's carrying, you need a fucking plan." He leaves me to it. Walking out the room and slowly closing the door behind him.

CHAPTER TWENTY-THREE

ARIA

ONE MONTH LATER

"Your son grows strong." Matteo's housekeeper, Anita, smiles at me as she places the sandwich, she's made me, on the coffee table. She's never really spoken to me before, so it comes as a surprise, it's an even bigger shock when she takes a seat beside me and places her palm, flat beside where mine rests on my stomach.

"Do you feel him wriggle yet, Miss Aria?" She smiles.

"No, the books said it could be any time now, but I don't feel him yet." I'm starting to get a little anxious about it. This past month my stomach has gotten much bigger, there is no hiding the fact I'm pregnant, now. We had an appointment with Doctor Fabier last week and heard his heartbeat again, and now I'm desperate to feel him move.

"Soon enough." She taps my bump, lightly, before she gets back up and heads into the kitchen. I look at the sandwich she's left behind and sigh when I think about eating it. Despite what Fabier, and the books, have said my nausea still hasn't passed, and I'm starting to wonder if I'll ever enjoy a meal again.

"Staring at it isn't going to make it disappear." Demitri laughs at me as he comes in from the patio. "You know Matteo is going to make you eat it?"

"Not if you eat it for me." I look up at him and smile.

"Oh, no." He shakes his head and laughs. "It would be more than my life is worth."

"Oh, come on, he won't even know." I drop my voice to a whisper.

"You know Anita makes the best sandwiches. Look at all that pastrami." I flit my eyes over toward the stuffed-full sandwich and bite my lip. You'd never know, from how appealing I'm making it sound, that it's making my stomach roll in disgust.

"I'll take one half." He points his finger at me, checking the coast is clear before he rushes at the plate and picks one up. Somehow, he manages to get almost a quarter of the thing in his mouth in one bite, and when Matteo walks through the door and catches him, he pauses mid-chomp.

"Hungry, Demitri?" Matteo raises his eyebrow.

"I...um..." Demitri struggles to get his words out around the mouthful of food he's got crammed in, so I speak for him.

"I asked him to test it, the meat smelt funny." I prove I've got his back and smile before burying my head back into the Pregnancy and Birth magazine Matteo brought home for me, yesterday.

"You think everything smells funny, these days." He steps closer, taking the magazine out of my hands and studying the article I'm reading about yoga.

"Shall I have Anita make you up something else?" He narrows his eyes on me, as he dismisses Demitri with his hand.

"No, I'm fine. I'm really not hungry." I know it isn't what

he'll want to hear but it's the truth, and I really can't stomach anything else after the huge breakfast he had me eat.

"You may not be, but the baby needs to be fed." He sits beside me and strokes his hand over my stomach.

"Does it look like I'm starving him? I've gotten huge. Nothing fits anymore, my belly pokes out of the bottom of all my tops." I look down at myself and pout.

"I've noticed, and I love it." Matteo slides his hand a little lower and strokes the bare skin, that my tee keeps riding up over.

"I'll have Anita get you some more clothes. There's a designer my mom knows who specializes in maternity wear, all the celebrities wear her."

"Don't you think that's a little overkill for me, just to slob around the house? It's not like I'll be going anywhere. I could just start wearing your sweats." I laugh, then stop myself when I notice how Matteo suddenly looks guilty. He sits forward on the couch, resting his elbows on his knees, and I can tell there's something he isn't telling me.

"What is it?" I slouch back and attempt to drag the tee, I'm wearing, down to cover my stomach, again.

"It hurts me too," he confesses, scrubbing his hand over his face. "There's nothing I want more, than to walk you out that door and show off to the world how beautiful you look, right now."

"Matteo, I wasn't—"

"You weren't, but it's true. This is no life for you, and yet it's the only one I can offer. Your dad hired a private investigator about a month ago. He ain't buying what you're telling him," he confesses, and suddenly everything starts to make sense. He's been even more tense than usual these past few weeks.

"And you didn't tell me about this? Matteo, I spoke to him just last week. He was frustrated, but he believed me."

"He's got my name on a list of suspects. All of them, people who they think may want to hurt you," he continues and when I sit back up, straight, and stare at him in shock, he looks even more guilty.

"And how many people are on that list?" I ask, unsure if I'm more shocked or scared to hear that.

"There were seven, now there's three." He turns his head so he's facing me, and I can tell by the look on his face that he's the reason it's shorter.

"Did you? Is that where you've been disappearing to?"

"Yes," he confirms, unapologetically.

"Matteo, they were just names on a list, I never felt threatened out there until..." I stop myself from continuing when I realize how bad it would sound.

"Until me," Matteo finishes my sentence for me, looking really hurt.

"I'm not gonna sit here and pretend you haven't changed me. I think we can both agree that's obvious. But, away from you and away from him," his eyes fall down to my stomach. "I'm still that ruthless bastard who dragged you away from the life you knew, and chained you in my basement." He presses a tight kiss on my cheek as he stands up.

"Eat the other half of that sandwich, Aria," he orders before walking away.

∼

I wake up to use the bathroom, and when I notice Matteo isn't there I instantly wonder if he's out taking another name off that list. He's been off ever since the discussion we had at lunchtime, and there is no doubt in my mind that someone out there will be suffering the rage he feels. It took me by surprise to hear that there are so many people out there who might want to hurt me but, then, I've always been a little delusional. It's easy to forget that you're a crime lord's daughter when you don't feel like anybody's daughter, at all.

I finish peeing and when I go to get back in bed my tummy actually growls at me. I realize that, for the first time in months, I haven't got that nasty, metallic taste in my mouth, anymore. In fact, I actually have a hunger for something. I just can't quite figure out what that something is. I lie staring at the ceiling for a few more minutes, worrying about where Matteo could be, right now. And when I come to the conclusion that I'm not gonna figure it out lying here and that my hunger isn't going anywhere, I get out of bed, throw on the vest that's far too small for me, along with a pair of Matteo's gym shorts and creep downstairs toward the kitchen.

It's strange that I feel so excited about actually being hungry; I keep the lights off so I don't wake any of Matteo's staff and head straight to the refrigerator. My eyes roam over the shelves looking for whatever it is my tastebuds want.

Since I've been pregnant Matteo has had Anita ensure there is plenty of different foods available, in the hope that there will come a time when I actually fancy something. I'll bet he'll be gutted not to be here to witness, for himself, how I intend to take full advantage of that fact.

I notice the bowl of lasagne that I figure is what I left at the dinner table, earlier. I'd managed to persuade Matteo that the salad and four new potatoes, I'd eaten, had filled me, and as tasty as Anita's home cooking is, it's not what I'm looking for, now. I find the punnet of strawberries and pull them out. Popping one in my mouth as I place them on the counter, and search for more things that appeal to me. I figure whipped cream will come in useful and I check the coast is clear before I take that out, shake it and spray it directly into my mouth. The satisfaction it brings makes me smile, and after I've gotten myself a little collection of random things to experiment with, I hoist my ass up onto the kitchen counter and start to tuck in, using the glow from the open refrigerator door. Strange ideas for the food in front of me start to combine themselves in my head, and I can't resist dipping my fingers into the pickle jar and pulling one out. The smell doesn't make my stomach roll the way I thought it might. I take the whipped cream and cover the tip of it, and just as I'm about to test if the theory in my head, that tells me it would be delicious, is right, the room slowly lights up. Looking out the front window I see the car headlights pull onto the drive and stare down, at the mess I've made, in panic.

"*Shit.*"

I quickly scramble off the counter when the room goes dark again, starting to gather everything up, but unable to resist ramming another strawberry in my mouth as I scoop up the evidence surrounding me.

"Fuck!" I curse when the can of whipped cream drops onto my toe, but I am impressed at my ability to protect the pickle I'm still holding, at all costs.

"Aria?" The kitchen light turns on brightly, and when I slowly turn my head and see Matteo standing in the doorway, all I can do is smile at him guiltily.

"What the hell is going on?" I can't think of a time when I've ever felt so embarrassed as I look around the mess I've made and watch his eyes focus on the cream-coated pickle, that's in my hand. He tries to hide his amusement behind his hand and I quickly turn my back on him.

"Don't look at me. I know I'm disgusting." I feel my cheeks heat up when I glance at the open peanut butter jar on the counter, that I just *had* to dip the strawberries in, too.

"Turn around." I hear his voice come from behind me,

sounding much closer than it did a few seconds ago. I do as he says, spinning on my feet and looking up at him.

"You've never looked fucking hotter than you do, right now." He uses his thumb to swipe something off my cheek, I'm guessing from the color of it that it's peanut butter and when he sucks it clean, I suddenly crave something very different to food.

Matteo says nothing as he crouches on the floor in front of me to retrieve the cream I dropped, and as he slowly works his way back up my body his free hand splays across my belly as he makes gentle kisses across it.

"You still hungry, Princess?" he asks, lifting the vest I'm wearing up over my tits and shaking the cream in his hand.

I nod, still clutching at the damn pickle, as he sprays cream over one of my nipples and smiles at me, darkly. He leaves it there as he slowly unbuttons his shirt, shrugging out of it and tossing it away, before he reaches behind me for the peanut butter and dips two of his fingers into the jar. I watch in fascination as he swipes them over my opposite nipple then, clutching both my tits together in his hands, he drops his head between them and sets his mouth to work. Feeling his tongue lap against me as he licks it off me, makes me moan and when I reach behind me to clutch the kitchen counter, I drop the pickle to the floor and fist my hands into his hair to keep him there.

I don't feel embarrassed any more, or hungry. All I can think about is the throb between my legs, that's building stronger, and how he's the cure to it.

Matteo's hands move behind me, sliding under the waist of his gym shorts and gripping my ass-cheeks before he drags them off my body and lifts me onto the kitchen counter.

My body is sticky, and his lips taste all kinds of weird when he kisses me

But I like it. I like it even more when I hear his buckle clink and feel his hard cock slide inside me. It doesn't matter how many times I've taken it, Matteo's cock always brings a little edge of pain when it first enters and I make that satisfied sound that I always do when he's fully inside me. Steadily, he pumps himself into me, taking my lip and dragging it with his teeth, and making me moan even louder as I slam my palm against the side of the refrigerator to brace myself for more.

Matteo fucks me a little harder than he has since I've been pregnant, and it feels so fucking good that my first orgasm comes embarrassingly quickly.

"That's right, pretty girl. You come for me," Matteo orders, gripping me harder as I clasp even tighter around him. "Your pussy feels fucking amazing," he whispers as his thrusts get harder. His head drops between us and he looks at my swollen stomach, affectionately, as he rests his hand over the ridge of it. "You're so fucking beautiful like this," he tells me. His cock feels so big inside me as each stroke, he makes, fills me to the hilt, and when I feel his body tense and his groans become louder, I know he's close.

"Get on your knees." He quickly pulls out of me and helps me off the kitchen surface, and I get to the floor just in time to catch the warm cum that spurts from his cock, on my tongue.

"That's right, you take that, Princess." I look up through my lashes at the satisfied look he wears as I lick him clean. "You look so fucking hot on your knees taking cock, with this cute, little belly sticking out." His hand reaches between us so he can stroke it, while the thumb from his other hand slides over my bottom lip, catching some of the cum that spills onto them and poking it back inside. I suck hard on his thumb as he feeds it to me. Then he shocks me when he grabs the pickle jar, and the cream from the work surface, and joins me on the floor. Resting his back against the kitchen cupboard and dragging me to sit between his legs.

"Were you really gonna eat that?" He nods his head at the pickle that I dropped on the floor.

"I was thinking about it." I blush.

"Okay." Matteo shrugs, unscrewing the lid of the pickle jar, taking one out and topping it off with cream. "Knock yourself out." He presents it in front of me and when I smile back at him over my shoulder I take it from his hands and lie back to rest my shoulders against his chest.

"You think I'm crazy, don't you?" I stare at it as my mouth waters to taste it.

"No, I'm just happy you're hungry." He makes a relieved sigh, and when I seize the day and bite into the pickle, I'm both astonished and delighted at how good it tastes.

"Mmmmm... you should try this," I tell him, holding my hand over my mouth as I chew.

"I'm good." He laughs to himself as he slides his hands around me so they frame my tummy and when I notice the blood flecks on his tan, leather shoes, I swallow my mouthful and wipe my hand over my mouth.

"Guess there's another name less on that list, huh?" I don't know if I feel relief, or sadness when I think about Matteo taking another life for me.

"There's only one name left on it now, Princess. And I can guarantee you he won't be hurting you, anytime soon." His thumbs stroke my stretched-out skin as he gently kisses my temple, and I can't help but find comfort in his words.

CHAPTER TWENTY-FOUR

MATTEO

I watch Aria in the reflection of my gym mirror, while I lift the dumbbells in my hands. Since I looked more into the article she was reading, the other day, about the benefits of yoga during pregnancy, I've had a mat brought up here so we can do our morning workout together.

She looks hot as shit in the training bra and yoga shorts she's wearing and the bigger her stomach grows, the more I seem to become obsessed with it. I feel a lot more relaxed, now that the list of people Fucchini's investigator thought could be a threat to her are dead; even more so now that she seems to have found her appetite, again. I swear that girl finds something new to dip a pickle into every day.

"You look real sexy when you're working out." She stares at me from the other side of the room like a vixen, then abandoning her mat she moves to sit on the weight bench beside me. I love how happy she looks when she leans back on one arm and the hand from her other strokes over her bump. Placing my weights back on the rack I position myself in front of her, taking her jaw between my thumb and finger and forcing her eyes to look up from her stomach and onto me.

"Do you like being pregnant?" I ask. Of course, there are things she moans about, but every now and then I catch her acting all dreamy, the way she is now.

"Surprisingly, I do," she nods back, almost seeming confused by her answer.

"Good, because I intend to knock you up many, more times. It looks too fucking good on you, for me not to." I lean down to kiss her, and when she glances toward the door, I see Demitri there, and I can tell from the look on his face that he hasn't come with good news.

"Can I get a word, boss?" he asks, gesturing his head to the hall.

"I'll be right back," I promise Aria, finishing that kiss I was giving her before I follow him out.

"What is it?" I ask once we're alone.

"The girl's father. He's here in L.A."

"What the fuck's he doing here?" His words come as a shock and I can already feel my heart starting to beat far too fucking fast.

"I don't know exactly. I got eyes on him. We're watching his every move. But I think we can pretty much guarantee that it's got something to do with her. The risk of him showing his face in your fucking city is too great for it not to be."

"What am I supposed to do?" I rub my hands over my face, exhausted from all this shit, just when things get back on track and I start to relax, something else creeps up on me.

"Like I said, boss, I got eyes on him, there isn't much else I can do."

I need to think straight and all this is far too pressing. I need to put some distance back, between me and Fucchini, and there's only one way I can think of to do that with the discretion I need.

"Have Marco get the jet ready. Tell him we're heading for the island."

"*The* island?" Demetri stares back at me in utter shock.

"Yes, Demitri, last I checked there was only one fucking island that would be any use to me."

"But you haven't been there since your dad—"

"I'm well aware of that," I march away from him and back to the gym room, where I find Aria on her knees with her back arched and her arms above her head. She must pick up on my sudden change of mood because she instantly looks worried.

It reminds me to find my calm again, I can't have her getting worried or stressed. It's bad for her and the baby.

"Is everything okay?" She stands up on her feet.

"Everything's fine, great in fact. We're going on a vacation," I announce, managing to smile.

"A vacation?" She seems completely startled by the idea. "Matteo, isn't that a little risky? You worry about us leaving the house to go to the doctor's office."

"Are you doubting me?" I snap back at her far too quickly, and when I notice her bottom lip start to pout, I quickly take her hand in mine, stroking it with my thumb and lowering my tone. "Where I'm taking you is secure, and very remote. You will be perfectly safe. Both of you." I assure her resting my hand on her stomach.

"I'll have Anita pack your bags for you. We'll be leaving in a few hours." I go to walk away but she pulls me back.

"All this seems very hasty, it's not like you to be so spontaneous." She creases her forehead.

"Everything is fine." I cradle her head in my hands and kiss the top of it, before leaving her and heading for my office. I shouldn't be around her when I'm on edge like this. Aria is very good at picking up on people's energy. The last thing I want is this one rubbing off on her.

. . .

Once I'm in my office with the door closed, I let my anger unleash, punching my fist at the wall and imagining it's Stevan Fucchini's fucking face. Demitri is right, he does know. I killed all those people on the list and left myself as the only suspect. I don't regret that, I wasn't going to allow people with any intent on harming Aria to roam out there, free. But now, there's a new threat. The threat of *him*. I slick back my hair and pull myself together before opening my door and calling out for Demitri. He's never far away, so he's with me almost instantly.

"Marco will meet you at the hangar in an hour," he assures me.

"Your contact, the one you had in Fucchini's house. I need you to get in touch, find out if they know why he's here, and how many men he's brought here with him." I can hear the panic in my voice, and realize I have to calm the fuck down because Aria thinks we're going on a fucking vacation.

"I haven't heard from my contact in weeks." Demitri hangs his head.

"*What?!*" I feel my blood start to boil.

"I've tried but haven't heard anything. I figure–"

"And you didn't think to give me the heads up on this?" I snap back at him, heading for the cabinet so I can pour myself something strong.

"You've been occupied, I'll remind you of the six-man rampage you insisted on doing all by yourself. I've never seen you like this, Matteo. I'm worried about you."

"Worried about me?" I laugh at him.

"I don't need you to worry about *me*, Demitri. I want you to worry about the safety of the woman who's carrying my child. If you'd have told me about your contact going MIA we could have predicted this. Now, I'm scratching around like a fucking mouse, running from my old goddamn city to an island I fucking detest!" I knock back my drink and take a seat behind my desk, my hand shaking as I stroke it over my mouth. I didn't mean to shout the way I just did, there's every chance Aria could have heard me and I don't want that.

"I'm sorry, Matteo," Demitri steps forward, looking guilty.

"It's not your fault, you can't say you didn't warn me this was a bad idea." I only have myself to blame for all this. Taking her *was* a bad idea, but watching her become even more beautiful, as her stomach swells with my child, makes it impossible for me to regret it.

"Leave with your girl, take a break on the island. Who knows, maybe she can help you find some beauty in it?" I look up at him doubtfully, and he smiles me a sad smile that confirms he knows, as well as I do, that I could never find beauty in that place.

"I will take care of everything, here. Like I said, I have eyes on Fucchini. Have the girl call him in a few days to give one of her updates and see what his reaction suggests."

"You're a good friend, Demitri." I let him know, before finishing the last of my drink and pulling myself together before I go to find her.

CHAPTER TWENTY-FIVE

ARIA

Something is troubling Matteo. I can tell by the way he keeps smiling at me. It's not like him, and it's not convincing at all. I take the sparkling water from the stewardess on his private jet and smile at her awkwardly while Matteo fixes the safety belt across my lap like I'm a child.

"I am capable of doing that myself you know," I remind him.

"I know, but if I do it, I can be assured that it's safe. He presses a kiss on my cheek and taps my tummy before looking up at the stewardess.

"That will be all," he dismisses her, taking my hand in his and looking out of the tiny window beside me.

"You never mentioned having a jet, or an island." I try to strike up a conversation in the hope that it might ease his tension,

"I don't visit it often." His lip curls like he has a nasty taste in his mouth.

"My father has an island too...but you already knew that, huh?" I look out the same window and inwardly curse myself when I realize I'm not helping the situation at all.

"Your father doesn't own his island, he just has access to it. Harold Fredimen owns the island my men took you from. He allows friends and people, who keep him rich, to use it as a perk," he corrects me.

"But, you own this island we're going to, right?" I check.

"My family has owned this island for decades."

"Then I can't wait to see it." I smile brightly, determined to lift his mood before we arrive.

I don't know how long we are in the air, I fell asleep not long after we took off, but when we do eventually get off the plane, the humidity hits me like a brick wall. I feel a little dizzy and shaky on my legs, as Matteo helps me down the steps and walks me toward the open-topped Jeep that's waiting for us. The runway is so tiny and surrounded by tropical forest that I'm surprised the pilot located it, and when I get into the passenger seat of the Jeep, I smile at Matteo and let him lean across me to pull my belt over my shoulder to buckle me in. As suffocating as he can be, it feels nice to have someone take care of me the way he does. He doesn't speak as he drives us over the bumpy track that leads through the trees, except to apologize for the roughness of the journey when I take a firm grip on the Jeep's roll bar.

Thankfully, we're only driving for a short time before we come to a clearing, and the uncomfortable journey becomes worth it when I see the white sandy beach and clear blue ocean in front of me.

"Home sweet home," Matteo utters under his breath, not sounding very enthusiastic, as he parks beside the luxury beach hut that looks out on the postcard-perfect view.

"Matteo, this place is beautiful." I unstrap myself and take his hand when he rounds the hood to help me out. The cove we're in is only small, but the mountains enclosing us are tall and luscious green from the trees that grow on them.

"Mr Romano." A female voice comes from the house, and when a short, older woman comes rushing toward us, I wonder where I recognise her from.

She greets Matteo with a warm hug that isn't reciprocated, then moves on to me, squeezing me tight, before holding me out in her arms and looking me over.

"Anita said you were pretty but you are quite beyond that." Her age-worn hand strokes my cheek.

"Aria, this is Grena, Anita's sister. She takes care of the house, here." Matteo introduces us, and I understand where I recognize her from. She has the same kind eyes her sister does.

"Everything is ready for you. I've already sent Emelle to the mainland for supplies so I can make you a good meal, tonight. I was thinking fish, it's brain food for the baby. Will that do, Mr Romano?" She smiles excitedly as her hand strokes my stomach.

"That will be perfect, Grena." He nods curtly.

"Thank you." I nod in agreement, noting how distant Matteo seems as he looks out at the ocean. He's brought me to paradise and yet, he seems haunted by it.

"Grena, please show Miss Aria to our room, I'm sure she is tired from our journey."

"Matteo." I clutch his hand and shake my head in confusion. I wish he would tell me what the matter is. Vacations are supposed to be fun, why would he bring me somewhere that makes him miserable?

"I have some calls to make, business back home doesn't stop because I take a vacation." He kisses my forehead lightly, before releasing his hand from mine and pulling his phone from his suit jacket. When he steps away for some privacy, Grena reminds me that she's still here when she takes my hand.

"Come, let me show you to your room, Miss Aria." Grena leads me toward the hut, and when I look over my shoulder, Matteo nods his head and offers me another one of his fake smiles to encourage me to go with her.

∽

"How can you be miserable here?" I pluck up the courage to ask Matteo when he eventually comes to our room. He's barely said a word to me since we arrived and he's spent all evening in his office. The four-poster bed, I'm lying on, looks out onto the ocean and the double doors are open to let in the cool, very welcome, evening breeze.

"I'm not miserable,' he assures me, taking off his cufflinks and placing them on the bedside table. I have no idea how he's managed to keep a suit on, in this heat. He even ate dinner, barefoot, with the bottom of his slacks rolled up, and I'm hoping that he's going to take a more casual approach during our time here. I wish I could say I was coping with the heat, as well as he is. I've had to have two showers since I've been here just to cool myself down, and I've already decided that I will be living in the bikini that Anita packed for me.

"Then start acting like you brought me on a vacation, then." I stand up on my knees and grab his tie, using it to tug him toward me. I loosen it enough to undo his top button, while I kiss him and he gives in to me easily enough, resting his hands on my hips and letting his tongue roll around mine as I slowly make my way through the rest of his buttons. When I'm done, he shrugs out of his shirt and takes hold of one of my thighs, his other hand reaching up my back so he can gently rest me back on the mattress. I know exactly where this is leading, and I don't care how hot it is, I'm here for it.

His fingers grip around my ankles, raising my feet so they

are flat on the bed with my knees bent and spread open in front of him. I almost make a joke about being in the same position for Dr Fabier last week, but I know he wouldn't find it very funny. He made it very clear that he didn't like how intrusive my check-up had been, and I got a very intense reminder of who my pussy belonged to after he had left.

I keep my mouth shut and watch as Matteo kneels to the floor and starts to kiss me through my panties.

Everything feels so heightened lately, I blush when I feel myself soak through them. But I can tell by the smile his lips make, as they press against me, that he likes it. When I start to buck my hips against his mouth something feral seems to come over him. He straightens up so he can use both hands to tear open the fabric barrier keeping us apart, then lowers back between my legs so he can lick me, tongue to flesh.

My fingers grip the bed sheet as his hands clutch my swollen belly and he looks over it, into my eyes, while he makes me come for him. I hope the walls aren't as thin as they look, and that Grena has her own place on the island when I shamelessly moan and thrash myself, uncontrollably, against his mouth.

"*Now* do you feel like you're on vacation?" he asks, kissing his way back up my body, giving extra care and attention to my nipples. They have been so sensitive since I've been pregnant, at first I struggled to have him touch them at all, but having his mouth surrounding them now sends a tingle of thrill all over my skin.

"Yes." I slide my fingers into his hair and gasp when I feel his hand slip between us and his fingers start to tease my entrance. My body fidgets desperately, to feel more of him, and he pulls back to watch me suffer, bracing himself on one of his hands, while his other makes me come all over again. I love that the smile on his face isn't fake anymore, it's a content one, and I return it when I get my breath back.

"You look stunning when you come for me," he whispers as his finger slips in and out of me, slowly, to wind me down; and I feel myself drench it even more when he stretches me open a little more and slips in another. "It hurts to look at you sometimes, you know that...?" His eyebrows hood over his eyes and I see that same hurt that's been with him all day, return. I want to question him over it, but I don't want him to stop doing what he's doing to me.

"Fuck me." I slide my fingers over his chest as I look down and watch the way I naturally ride both his fingers. "Fuck me hard like you used to." I hear the desperation in my voice, and as much as I know he wants to be gentle with me, I see that same desperation in Matteo's eyes. He may think he's a closed book, but he doesn't fool me.

"I can't." He shakes his head, straining his neck when he looks up at the ceiling like he's praying to God to give him the power of resistance.

"You won't hurt me and I promise, if you did, I'd tell you. I just want you to fuck me the way you used to. I miss it and, right now, you need it."

"Aria, I can't," he answers through gritted teeth. His fingers starting to become a little less gentle as they fuck me.

"Please, Matteo. *I* need it too."

I hear him growl in frustration when he moves away from the bed, and just when I think he's going to storm off, he shocks me when he roughly unbuckles his belt.

I smile victoriously as I watch him undress and see the harsh threat on his face as he comes back toward me.

"You make me go against my better judgment," he tells me, looking between my legs. "Look at this pussy." He tilts his head and admires what's laid out in front of him before he forces my knees even further apart. "Weeping so desperately over my bed sheets, throbbing to be filled with my cock." I nod back at him unashamedly, that's exactly what's happening, and I can tell from the darkness in his eyes that he's about to give me exactly what I want. Though, I really don't expect what comes next. Matteo's fingers land sharp and hard between my legs, spanking my pussy, and making me gasp from the unexpected thrill that comes from it. "I fucking love this pussy, Aria. I love it even more when it's desperate." He lowers his head and licks me right through my seam, then spitting sharply at my clit, he studies his finger as he uses it to mix his saliva with my pleasure.

"Look at your pretty, little face. I can see the fucking ache you're feeling, all over it; your desperation to feel me inside you is unmistakable." He teases me even more when he takes his cock in his hand and lets it slip between my pussy lips. "So fucking close, but not quite there, huh, Princess? I'll bet I could make you come like this. With my cock, edging closer and closer, to where you need it."

I nod back at him, managing to see over the curve of my stomach how it looks as he slides it agonizingly, slowly through my pussy lips.

"I'm going to give you want, Aria," he assures me, stroking my cheek with his thumb and swiping away some hair that's stuck to my cheek. "Just give me what *I* want first. I want to feel this needy, little clit throb against my cock before I fill you with it." He moves so slowly that my body aches from the anticipation. "In three..." He spits at the tip of his cock to soak it some more. "Two..." His thick head touches that sweet spot... "One." His stern voice tips me over the edge, and I give him exactly what he requested. It feels so intense. Like my entire body is being squeezed in a vice, and just when I'm about to scream out his name, he shocks all the breath out of me when his cock slips inside me and he fills me in one long stroke.

"*Fuuuck!*" The words tumble from my mouth and when I feel Matteo's hand grip around my throat, I take hold of his wrist so he'll keep it there. It's been too long since we've had it like this. I appreciate how gentle he's been with me, but I miss the man he was before he got me pregnant. That savageness is back in his eyes as he fucks me, deep and hard, and it confirms he's got something heavy on his mind. I stare back at him, searching into his soul and begging for him to share whatever it is with me, but everything becomes too intense, and I lose control of my mind as well as my body. My legs shake, my heart thumps and my shattered body gives into yet another orgasm as Matteo thrusts his huge, hard cock inside me faster, and harder than I've had it for months. I know he's close when his fingers clench my throat tighter.

"Mine!" he growls, fucking me frantically. "No one will *ever* fucking take you from me, Aria."

He makes one long, final push inside me and I feel the force of his cum as it unleashes.

There's nothing but the sound of the waves lapping outside and our breathing, as he slowly trails his hand away from my neck and uses it to hold himself over me on the mattress without crushing my middle.

"Matteo." I manage to find my voice, and when I look up at him he drops his head in shame. His shoulders rise and fall, rapidly, while he catches his breath.

"I shouldn't have done that." I can tell by the low tone in his voice that he's mad at himself.

"I needed you to," I admit, taking his cheek in my hand and guiding his eyes back up to mine. "*You* needed to," I remind him.

"You have no fucking idea how precious you are, do you?"

He shakes his head and narrows his eyes at me. "I don't deserve you. I don't deserve what you're giving me." His eyes lower between our bodies and focus on my growing stomach. "I have to keep you both safe. I can't lose either of you."

"You aren't going to lose us. We're right here," I assure him.

"Matteo, please tell me what's wrong. Tell me why we're really here." He closes his eyes and sighs before sliding his cock out of me and laying back on the mattress beside me. We both look up at the bamboo ceiling in silence and I'm just about to ask him again when his voice silences me.

"Your father is in L.A.," he confesses, in a weak voice that proves how worried he is.

"What?" I turn my head to face him, doing nothing to hide my shock.

"He arrived last night, according to Demitri. I don't know what he wants, but there's a strong chance it could be you and I won't let that happen." He rolls onto his side and props his head on his hand.

"Aria, I'm never gonna let you go. Not even if you wanted to. I would keep you a prisoner if I had to because I'm addicted to you." His words should scare me, but they don't.

"That's why we're here because there are very few people who know about this island, all of them are people that I trust. I'll keep you here for as long as I have to. I will not let your father take you back."

"So, I guess we'll just have to suffer here, in paradise." I smile back at him, trying to lighten the mood. Of course, I'm worried about my father's sudden appearance in L.A., but Matteo is always telling me stress isn't good for our baby. I can see he's going above and beyond to make sure we're safe. I have every faith in him.

"Trust me, this place is a long way from paradise." He looks down at his finger as it draws slow, delicate circles around my belly button. "There's nothing but bad memories for me here. I would never have dragged you both out here unless I had to."

"You wanna talk about it?" I ask, intrigued by his attitude toward this place.

"Never." He smiles sadly, before shimmying down the bed so he can press soft kisses all over my stomach.

"You think he's okay? I lost control." His hand strokes the underside of my tummy, affectionately.

"He's fine," I assure him, smiling to myself when I feel that fluttering sensation I've been getting, just lately. It's nothing that can be felt from the outside, and I can't be entirely sure it's him, but it feels amazing when it happens.

"And what about you? I don't know how long we're gonna have to wait this out. Can you be comfortable here, until I do?" He looks up at me.

"I'll be fine as long as we're together." I stroke his hair out of his eyes and smile.

CHAPTER TWENTY-SIX

MATTEO

I see his blood soaking into the sand as his wide-open eyes stare right into my soul.

"Good job, son." My father squeezes my shoulder as my shaky hand lowers the gun I'm holding.

"Good job," he repeats, leaving me to stare at the man I just killed, and walking back toward the beach house. I notice him stop and say something to Mom, from the corner of my eye. I can't hear over the sound of the ocean what it is but she doesn't respond to it. She just looks numb as she sits on the step with a crystal glass of vodka in her hand and a blank look on her face. She's shaking, just like me, and I've never seen her cry before, but the thick, black heavy tears that have run through the make-up she's wearing are unmistakable.

"You made him proud, kid." Demitri's father, Gino, gives me a reassuring nod, as he and another one of my father's guards lift the body off the sand and place it in a long, black body bag. And when I look across the beach and see my best friend watching me too, I wonder if today's the day he's feeling lucky not to be me.

. . .

"Matteo. Matteo...Quick!" Aria shakes me awake, and the urgency in her tone has me shooting off my pillow to sit up.

"Is it the baby?" I quickly check her over, starting to panic.

"Yes," she nods back at me but doesn't seem to look concerned. In fact, she looks really fucking happy.

"Give me your hand." She reaches out for it, then guides it toward her stomach, placing my palm flat against her sexy, little bump.

"He's strong enough for you to feel too." She smiles adorably at me as I feel a tiny ripple move beneath my palm. "I've been feeling these flutters for a few weeks now, but you feel that too, right?" she checks.

"Yeah, I...I feel it." I stare at my hand, willing to feel it again, and when it eventually happens we both laugh at the same time.

"That's our little boy." She bites her bottom lip like she's holding back tears, and I stroke my hand gently across her stomach wondering if he can feel me too.

"Does it feel strange?" I ask, trying to imagine what it must be like for her. We've been on the island almost two weeks, and I swear her neat, round bump gets bigger with each day that passes. She gets even sexier with it too.

"Yeah, but a good strange. It feels kind of magical." I get such a kick out of seeing how happy she is, and for the first time since I took her from her life and put her into mine, I don't feel guilty.

"Thank you." I look into her pretty, blue eyes as my thumb strokes over her.

"For what?" She laughs at me through those happy tears that she just can't hold in.

"For giving me my first ever, happy memory on this island." I don't want to think about the past, especially not now. Aria just pulled me out of a nightmare and placed a dream right in my hand. It gives me even more determination to do things right.

"You wanna make another one?" A spontaneous idea comes into my head and I jump out of bed and hold my hand out for her.

"Always." Aria smiles at me through her lashes, taking a little more time than she used to, to get up from the bed. She doesn't question me, she just makes that sweet, little giggle as I drag her through the patio doors and lead her out toward the Jeep.

"Matteo, I have no shoes on." She laughs and when it reminds me of my carelessness, I pause to lift her up in my arms and carry her the rest of the way.

"Where are we going?" she asks when I place her carefully in the passenger seat and strap her in, then rushing around to get behind the wheel I start the engine.

"It's a secret," I tell her, quickly pulling away and heading for a spot I know she's going to love.

Thankfully, the moon is full enough for me to be able to appreciate the look on Aria's face when we get to the falls. The water sparkles from the silvery-blue glow above it, and the sky is clear enough for the stars to provide us some light too.

Aria doesn't say anything, just stares around us in awe as I help her out of the Jeep and lead her to the water's edge.

"You wanna take a swim?" I reach over my back and pull my tee over my head, before stepping out of my boxers and kicking them aside.

"You serious?" She stares back at me like I've lost my mind.

"I'm really fucking serious." I hook my fingers into the waistband of the cute, little boy shorts she's wearing and drag her closer.

"This isn't like you." She shakes her head in confusion, but the smile rooted on her face suggests she's loving it. I've been on edge and hard to be around since we got here, I get that. But feeling my son move around inside her tonight, has reminded me what I'm here for.

"Maybe, it's something you bring out in me," I tease, raising the tight vest top that sits just above her tummy, up over her tits, and lifting it off her head. Her nipples instantly harden from the cool, evening air, and when her cute, little smile turns into a daring one, she sets to work pushing her shorts down to her ankles and stepping out of them.

I take her hand and lead her into the water, pleasantly surprised at how warm it is, and when we make it up past our waists, I turn our bodies so we're facing each other and curl my hands under her ass to lift her onto me. Her stomach doesn't allow me to hold her as close as I used to be able to, and when she rests her arms on my shoulders and lets her fingers cross behind my neck, she stares at me dreamily.

"I like you like this. I mean, I like you when you're a grump too, but when you're like this–" I kiss her lips to stop her from saying anything else I don't deserve, and my cock naturally finds its position near her entrance.

She looks so perfect, lit up by the reflection of the moonlight that comes off the water, and when I reach my hand under the water and guide my cock slowly inside her, the satisfaction on her face makes me feel like the luckiest man in the world.

This woman should hate me for who I am, my plan could have destroyed her life and yet here she is, so grateful and proud to have my child growing inside her and doing such a good job of it.

"That's really nice," she whispers as I gently rock myself inside her, kissing her neck as the water laps around us.

"Marry me." The words seem to come out all by themselves but I don't regret them. Aria belongs to me, and I want her to have the Romano name like our child will.

"Yes." Her instant answer makes me pause, and I pull back my head so I can check I heard her right. "Don't look so shocked. Of course, I want to be your wife." She makes it all sound so simple.

"Okay, I'll make it happen." I kiss her softly as I slowly fuck her in the water and when we both come at the same time, her anticipating little breaths turn into a desperate moan. I love the way our bodies are in sync with each other now, and for a long time, after I've filled her pussy with more of my cum, I hold her as tight to me as I can get her.

"You cold?" I check when I eventually drag my cock from her tight pussy. It suddenly dawns on me what a stupid idea this was. I have no towels to keep her warm or dry her skin when we get out of this water

"I'm fine." She shakes her head at me.

"You won't be if you get a chill. Now, you're gonna get cold and–"

"He's moving again," she interrupts me, taking my hand and placing it back on her stomach so I can feel it too.

"See Matteo, we're fine. You're doing a great job of taking care of us." I didn't realize it till just now, but her words are exactly what I needed to hear. And suddenly this island, that I didn't want to bring her to, seems like the place I want to keep her, for the rest of her life.

"Come on, let's get you home." I kiss her one more time before dragging her out the water and using my tee to dry her off the best I can.

CHAPTER TWENTY-SEVEN

ARIA

Matteo meant what he said when he told me he'd make our marriage happen, it's only been five days since he proposed to me at the waterfall, and today the beach is all set up for our private ceremony. Demitri is flying to the island with the marriage certificate he somehow arranged for us, and, since Matteo is insistent that we do things right, he's bringing a priest with him. I've never had him down as the religious type, but I'm a go-with-the-flow kind of girl.

"Are you nervous?" Grena asks as she adds a few more pins to my hair.

"Not at all, it's not like there's a lot of people here for me to mess my vows up, in front of." I smile back at her through the mirror, as she places the pretty, purple orchid among the neat up-do she's given me.

"Oh, sweetheart, marriage is about far more than just the vows. It's about a love in your heart that overflows. It's perseverance against all odds. Marriage is not easy. Especially, to a man like Matteo Romano." She smiles and steps back so she can admire her work.

"I do love him, you know. We aren't just getting married

because of the baby." I stroke my bump affectionately, it's too big to hide now and sticks out rather prominently from the white dress Matteo had shipped over, with the rest of the supplies from the mainland.

"I see that, I have known Matteo for a lot of years and I've never seen him be the way he is, with you, to anyone." She smiles.

"So, you've always been on the island." I see an opportunity to find out what troubles Matteo so much about this place.

"Yes, the late Mr Romano resided here, toward the end. Matteo pays me to keep the place nice, even though he hasn't visited since his passing." She smiles sadly, patting down the bed to try and make herself look busy.

"How long ago was it?" I ask, getting up from the dresser stool and helping her fluff the pillows.

"Please, Miss Aria, rest."

"I don't want to rest. I spend all day resting. I want to know about this place. I want to know why Matteo didn't want to come here," I admit.

"I like the way you make him smile." Grena ignores everything I've just said as she strokes my cheek like a proud mother. "I'll see you on the beach." She leaves me alone with my thoughts. I stand in front of the mirror and look at my reflection, wondering how my life could have changed so much, in such a short time.

Our baby boy wriggles inside me and I stroke my hand over where he moves. I'm feeling him more and more now, and Matteo has spent hours with his hand resting on my stomach, feeling him too. He's fascinated by the changes that are happening to my body, and although everything seems a little hasty, it feels right that we're doing this. I just wish Matteo wouldn't keep things from me.

"Can I come in?" I hear Matteo's voice come from the door and quickly spin around.

"You're not supposed to see me before the wedding," I remind him.

"I'm not superstitious, are you?" he checks, walking toward me and admiring how I look in my dress.

"You look beautiful." He smiles down at the hand he has stroking my swollen belly before his eyes pick back up to fix on mine.

"I wanted to give you something." He reaches into his back pocket and pulls out a small red box.

"I never made our engagement official," he explains.

"That's because it only lasted a few days." I laugh at him, only Matteo Romano could put together a wedding on a remote island in less than a week.

"That is irrelevant, every bride should have an engagement ring." He opens the box to reveal the antique-style ring with a diamond on it so big, I'm sure it'll weigh me down.

"This was my grandmother's ring, her and my grandfather lived a long and happy life together. He made her very happy, and it will always be my intention to do the same with you."

"It's perfect." I stare at it, mesmerized, as he takes it from the box and slides it onto my finger.

"Not nearly as perfect as you, but it will do." His hand cradles my face and I naturally lean into it.

"Demitri tells me that your father has bought an apartment in downtown L.A. He intends to stay," he admits, sounding disappointed.

"Does that mean we can't go home?" I don't know if the thought of that gives me relief or fills me with dread. I like the seclusion of the island but we only have three months before the baby is due to come.

"It just means we have to stay here a little longer, and

maybe I will need to make changes to my plan for when the baby comes." He smiles again when he mentions our baby, albeit a sad one this time.

"Okay." I nod back, letting him know I trust his judgment. Grena is right, a marriage is about more than just the vows we will make today. Although his original intentions were selfish, I see a different man, to the one who took me, standing in front of me now. I see a man I want to spend the rest of my life with.

"Are you ready to become Mrs Romano?" His soft touch turns firm, as he grips my jaw tight in his fingers and draws me closer to his lips.

"I sure am." I press my mouth against his, before grabbing the pretty bouquet Grena made for me and heading out to the beach with him.

∽

The ceremony was much faster than I imagined it would be, which given the heat, I'm grateful for, and the surprise appearance of Matteo's mother came as quite the shock. After Matteo kisses me in a way that is not suitable in front of a priest, we walk hand in hand down the aisle made from pretty flowers and palm leaves. Demitri offers me a courteous nod as we pass him, while Mrs Romano gets up from her chair and blocks our path.

"Congratulations." She plants a cold kiss on my cheek before reaching up to hug her son.

"I'm glad you could make it." Matteo doesn't sound at all genuine as he quickly moves us past her, and straight into the house, closing the double doors and pulling down the bamboo blind to shut them all out.

"Matteo, what are you doing? We have guests…" I shake my head in disbelief when he starts undoing his tux jacket, shrugging out of it and tossing it at the floor. He comes at me slowly and with that stern look of determination in his eyes.

"I'm going to fuck my wife." He reaches his hand under my dress and grips at my panties, ripping them down to my ankles.

"But your mother's out there, there's a priest waiting for a lobster dinner, for Christ's sake!"

"I don't care." He lifts me by my thighs and slams my ass onto the dresser, positioning himself between my legs.

"They'll know what we're doing." I push my hand against his chest to force him away.

"I'll invite them in here to watch if that's what they want." He shoves my hand away before unbuckling his belt and taking out his cock. It's already rock hard, and the tip of it glistens with pre-cum as he lets it rest on my stomach.

"Matteo, they'll be waiting for us."

"Then we better make this quick. Then we go back out, do the polite shit with them, and I send them on their way, so I can spend the rest of the evening making you come." He pushes my dress up over my belly, smothering it with his hands as his cock lines itself up with my entrance and he pushes inside me, obliterating any fight or argument I had against him.

"How does it feel to take your husband's cock?" He pulls out and thrusts back inside me, gradually getting faster, until the dresser I'm resting on rattles against the thin, structured walls.

"Incredible," I answer, looking down between our bodies. My stomach is too big for me to see him entering me, but the way his hands caress it so possessively as he fucks me makes me even wetter for him.

"You are a Romano now, Aria. You belong to me."

"I've *always* belonged to you." I look back up at him so he knows I mean what I say. I've felt owned by this man since the day I first saw him in his basement. My pussy tenses tight around him and my first orgasm, as a married woman, comes out with a loud moan as I push back against his thrusts and ride it out.

"Jesus, I'm gonna come." He quickly pulls out, landing his hard, heavy cock on my stomach and spilling all over my skin. He drops his forehead on mine, breathing heavily, as his hand rubs his warm, sticky mess into my skin the same way as he does the cocoa butter after I've bathed.

"I fucking love you, Aria Romano," he tells me, tapping his still-solid cock against my stomach to shake off the last of his cum.

"That's the first time you've ever told me that." I look at him and smile, as a warm tingle spreads through my chest.

"Well, get used to it, you're gonna hear it plenty more." He presses a kiss to my lips. "Come, we should entertain our guests."

I smile at him as he helps me off the dresser. "Just give me a few minutes to wash this off, I'll be right out." I start to head for the bathroom, but he drags me back.

"Naha. I want you wearing that on your skin all the way through dinner." He pulls my dress back over my belly and smoothes it out, neatly.

"I'll clean you up in the bath later when I've finished fucking you." Retaking my hand, he moves us toward the door and this time I pull him back.

"I love you too," I tell him, realizing that I didn't say it back. I don't know why, but I get the impression he hasn't been told it many times before.

CHAPTER TWENTY-EIGHT

MATTEO

"What are you doing out here all alone?" I turn my head away from watching the ocean when I hear her voice come from behind me. I thought she'd be flat-out asleep after all the different ways I've made love to her since our guests left the island.

"Couldn't sleep." I shrug, continuing to watch the waves slide onto the sand and drag back out, again.

"We could talk about whatever's on your mind?" She sits down beside me, burying her feet in the sand as I wrap my arm around her shoulders.

"Some things are better left unsaid." I kiss the top of her head and smell her hair, despite the coconut undertone of her shampoo, she smells of me, and I love it.

"I disagree, I think whatever it is that's on your mind would feel much better if you shared it. Are you scared about my father being in L.A.?"

"I'm not scared of your father, Aria." I shake my head. "I told you, I'm figuring all that out."

Aria called Stevan last week and the fact he hasn't told her he's in L.A., and he wasn't as pressing with her about where she was, makes me even more certain that he knows she's with me. But he is not what I've got on my mind, tonight.

"Okay, so if it's not my father that's keeping you awake, what is it?"

"Just old memories." I smile to myself, sadly.

"You must have had some good memories here. You said your family have always owned this place. Did you visit as a child?" She sounds so optimistic and innocent, and I don't want to spoil that. Demitri's right, this version of myself is only for her. But, to anyone else, I am unchanged. Aria Romano deserves to know what kind of man she's really married to.

"Yeah, I visited here as a child. I killed my first man, right over there, by those rocks." I point my finger over to the other side of the beach and when Aria twists her head back to look at me all the optimism has gone from her face.

"We came out here one summer for some family time. Just before we got here, Dad found out that Mom had been screwing her personal trainer. He had him flown out here a few days later as a surprise for her." I swallow the lump in my throat when I remember her shocked face. Father had told us over breakfast that he had a gift for her, then had Gino drag her lover, bound and gagged, into the room. Aria takes hold of the hand I've got hanging over her shoulder and squeezes it tight.

"He had me shoot him, right in front of her," I explain, hearing her breath catch in shock. "It was the first time I'd ever killed anyone, and I remember the fear in that man's eyes when I pulled the trigger." I hate how weak I sound, and how her eyes are pitying me now.

"That's an awful thing to make a child do. How old were you?"

"I was ten, and the worst part about it is that at the time, the person I was most mad at was my mom."

"And now?" Aria asks, sounding intrigued.

"Now, I see it for what it really was, it was all part of the games my dad liked to play. He had loads of different women. Mom would turn a blind eye to it all, he'd bring his mistresses to this island and leave Demitri's father, Gino, in charge back home. I've seen him cheat on my mom more times than I can remember. What he did that day made me realize that I could never be a normal kid, or grow up to have a normal life. It was a test, and over the years he gave me many more."

"So, that's why you hate it here so much," she whispers softly.

"That's part of the reason. I'm not gonna sit here and lie to you, Aria. Killing men doesn't bother me, any more, there are times I even get a sick little kick out of it. Like when I killed Dennis Jefferson, and those men on that list. But the last thing my dad asked me to do was the hardest." I look up at the stars and remember looking up at the same constellation that night. The air was thick and sticky just like it is now, and suddenly my pulse starts beating the same way it did, five years ago.

"What happened, Matteo?" Aria can't hide the worry from her eyes as she twists her body more into mine.

"Dad was really ill for the last few years of his life, he had all kinds of specialists look at him, and no one could help. For a long time, he managed to cover it up. Him and Mom were still married but living separate lives and he spent all his time out here. Me and Gino were running things back home. Then one day, he summoned me out here. I was really shocked when I saw him and realized how bad he'd gotten." I can still remember the paleness of his skin and how it sagged from his bones. He'd looked like a corpse, already. "He told me there was no life for him, anymore, that the pain had become unbearable and he asked me to take it away."

"He asked you to kill him?" I watch her eyes widen.

"Yeah," I admit, letting the sand slide through the fingers of my free hand.

"Matteo...?"

"I got that he wanted to die, anyone could see he was in pain."

"But to ask that of your son..." She shakes her head, still stunned.

"Well, that was him for you, looking to teach a lesson in any way he could." The laugh I make isn't done out of humor, it comes from deep-rooted sadness that I can't believe I'm actually sharing with her.

"He told me a lion who wants to take over the pride, would have to kill to take his spot, he said the job was mine and no one else's. It was my responsibility to carry it out."

"And did you?" I'm pretty sure Aria already knows the answer, but I give her the courtesy of one, anyway.

"I did. I held a pillow over his face, and I ended him." I think back to the way his body thrashed against me, his survival instinct using the last of his strength to try and fight me off. In that moment, I used all the hate I'd built for him over the years to force that pillow down harder and when his last breath left his body, I didn't feel a shred of remorse.

"Matteo, that must have been awful." Aria's eyes fill with tears of sympathy.

"Yeah, well, it's done now. I carried out what he wanted. I never *did* let him down when he wanted a job done." I wipe the lone tear from my eye and hope she doesn't notice it.

"I want to do things differently. No fucking games." I slide my hand over her stomach and smile when I feel our son fidget under my palm.

"You're a different man to the one I first met," she tells me, placing her hand over mine and looking up at me. Somehow, this girl has always seen the good in me, even when it hasn't been there.

"Thank you for sharing with me what happened. I don't like the idea of us having secrets from each other." Her eyes drop down to our hands when our baby moves, again.

"We're going to make this a happy place, from now on. No looking back at old memories, just happy ones," she promises. And I nod my head because I'm totally good with that.

CHAPTER TWENTY-NINE

ARIA

"Everything is progressing perfectly." Dr Fabier finishes pressing his hand into my pelvis to check the baby's position and steps over to the dresser, where his notes are. I can't imagine how much it must have cost Matteo to fly him out here, it seems over the top considering there are perfectly good doctors less than an hour's boat ride away, on the mainland.

"But..."

"What do you mean 'but'?" Matteo stands himself up straight from where he's been resting his shoulder against the patio door frame, watching my examination, sternly.

"Unless you plan on having this baby here on the island, which I wouldn't recommend, you will have to start making plans for a return to the mainland." He clears his throat as if he can sense it's not what Matteo wants to hear.

"Aria is only five weeks away from her due date, it's not recommended that a pregnant mother fly any less than four," he adds, causing Matteo to run his finger across his lip and nod like he's known this was coming. Then he rushes over to help me when I struggle to get myself up into a seating position on the bed.

"I will remain on call, but if something were to happen here, there is no guarantee I would make it here on time, nor do you have the facilities for the event of complications." The way he refuses to look either of us in the eye when he says that, is just a reminder that the majority of people are terrified of my husband.

"Thank you. I'll be sure to make those arrangements." Matteo looks stressed as he marches out the door, sliding his hand through his hair the way he always does when he's mad, and leaving me and the doctor alone. With him gone, I see an opportunity.

"What kind of complications could there be?" I want to know so I can be prepared.

"Most births go completely to plan, especially when the mother is as healthy as you are. I see nothing that gives me any concern or reason to doubt that you should–"

"But...what are the risks of me delivering here, on the island?" I rush him to the point, putting on a brave face and pretending not to be scared.

"Well, for a start, there would be no pain relief, not all women require it, but many do–"

"That's not a complication. I want to know the risks!" I cut him off.

"Sometimes, the baby isn't in the correct position for birth, a breech baby can be very hard to deliver, especially without medical assistance. Your baby is already head down, but there's nothing to say that may change. There are risks of placenta abruption and...Look, there are many risks, Aria. My strong advice is for you to leave this island and return home, or at least go somewhere close to a medical center." He places his hand over mine and smiles curtly before grabbing his medical bag and following Matteo out.

Matteo has hidden himself away in his office and I figure, given the mood he was in when he left the bedroom, I should give him his space. Instead, I take a book out onto the porch and somehow manage to get myself into the hammock. I lose myself in the story I'm reading, and with the warm glow of the sun on my face I eventually drift off to sleep.

I don't know how long I was napping for, but I wake up to his fingers stroking softly over my swollen stomach as I sway, and when I open my eyes the smile on his face looks almost guilty.

"I didn't mean to wake you," he whispers. "You just looked so beautiful I had to come over and touch you." I look down at my body and roll my eyes. My stomach sticks out like a beach ball, you can barely see the orange bikini bottoms I'm wearing, and my tits have become so big and heavy they spill out of my bikini top. Which is the only thing I seem to feel comfortable in, with this heat.

"Well, I feel like an elephant," I assure him, supporting my belly as I twist into a better position.

"I've been thinking…" Matteo sighs heavily

"About us going home?" I can see how hard this is for him.

"You heard what the doctor said, staying here isn't an option." He drops his head and focuses on his hand when our son kicks.

"I have to protect you both, and I don't know how to do that with your father so close. You don't know him like I do, Aria, he doesn't play fair."

"This isn't a game Matteo, this is something we have to face up to. We have our story, he doesn't need to know you took me. We're married now, he can't just take me away from you." I try my best to assure him, but I can see it isn't working.

"I ordered for the jet to come back tomorrow morning. Tonight's going be our last night here," he tells me sadly.

"Then we better make it count." I wiggle my eyebrows at him.

"Do you ever think of anything else, these days?" I can see his mood has already shifted when he huffs a laugh at me.

"Other than my husband's big cock? Not really." I shrug, shrieking in shock when his arms slide under me and lift me from the hammock.

"What are you doing?" I giggle as he carries me back inside the house.

"I'm making it count." He kisses me.

CHAPTER THIRTY

MATTEO

"It seems strange being back home doesn't it?" Aria smiles, as we walk through the door to my mansion. She's right, being here does feel strange, especially knowing her father is here in the city, and all I can do is try to remain calm for her.

"You should go and rest, all the traveling must have tired you out." I place a kiss on her cheek and smile at her, assuringly.

"You're home!" Anita bursts through the kitchen door with a welcoming smile and does me an unintentional favor when she sweeps Aria off into the living room, asking to hear all about our wedding.

I look at Demitri, who's standing on the other side of the hall, and gesture to my office. He quickly follows me, closing the door behind him.

"So, what do we know?" I ask, pouring myself a drink, and letting my frustration release. Suddenly, the island and all the new memories we made there seem a million miles away.

"Fucchini has made some investments while he's been here, ones that suggest he'll be sticking around."

"What *kind* of fucking investments, Demitri?" I slam my

hand at the table in frustration. There has only been one other time in my life that I've felt so helpless and that was when the car, that drove the woman who was carrying my child, blew up right in front of me.

"He's invested big on some luxury apartment project."

"Property?" I shake my head, doubtfully. Stevan Fucchini is known for making his money from contraband, not bricks and mortar.

"I know, it seemed strange to me too, but that's what I'm hearing."

"And how about things here, are they running smoothly?" I start sifting through the unopened mail on my desk.

"Everything is fine, I had a meeting with our Columbian importer just last week, he assures me he can keep up with our demand for supply."

"What is this?" I hold up the cream-colored envelope with my name neatly calligraphed on the front. "You know I don't accept invitations, they shouldn't even make it onto my desk. You always decline on my behalf." I toss the envelope across my desk at him, and the clever smile he gives me back suggests I've missed something.

"I think you might make a special exception for this one." He presses his finger on top of it and slides it back in front of me.

"Your mother has arranged a get-together at her house so you and Aria can announce your marriage. She's also invited Aria's father," he explains

"*What!*" I slam both my palms onto my desk and lean over it. "And you're just telling me about this, now?"

"I was sworn to secrecy, by your mother."

"I'm sorry, Demitri, I must have missed the memo that told me you were working for her, now."

"I work for you. I care for you, and I see you like a fucking brother. Your mother has organized a safe environment for you both to come clean to Aria's father. There will be witnesses and guards surrounding the place. I didn't tell you, because I knew you would act this way, and I think it's a good idea."

"You think taking my eight-month pregnant wife to a party where the man who's been trying to find her is going to be, is a good idea? Demitri, she's going to freak out over this. She's too close to her time to be worrying about this shit."

"She's not going to freak out," Demitri assures me.

"Oh, yeah, and how can you be so sure?"

"Because the whole plan was her idea. She came up with it on the day of the wedding." He scratches his neck, nervously.

"That was over a month ago." I rip open the envelope and read the invitation.

"She called your mom yesterday when she found out you were coming home and Vivian put her plan into action."

"So, Stevan Fucchini is just expected to come up to my mother's home, the wife of his rival and grandmother of the child he murdered?" I lower my voice into a harsh whisper for that last part. Aria doesn't know about what her father did, and I've decided that she never will. I may have taken her away from him, but I will give her the privilege of at least believing the man, who created her, isn't a monster.

"That is yet to be determined. The invitations only went out this morning. I guess if he believes you have his daughter he will attend out of curiosity."

"I don't fucking like this at all," I growl, scrubbing my face as the anxieties build up inside me. "Having him, and her, in the same room is too much of a risk."

"We will have enough security, Fucchini is coming onto our territory. Aria will be safe. This is what she wants, Matteo. Your plan for vengeance on the man failed when you fell in love with her, now all you can do is find some kind of resolution moving forward." He shrugs, with that told-you-so look on his face.

"And when is this party?" I glance over the invitation and see for myself that it's next Friday. "Do you think we can keep her here, safe until then, what if he plans to attack here, to get her?"

"Like I said, our security is tight, you saw how many guards there are out there. Fucchini is in *our* town, I've had him watched, he only has one man with him," he assures me.

"Reply. Tell Mother we'll be there." I fling the invitation back at the table and march out my office, trying to tamp down my anger before seeking out my wife.

I find her resting on the couch with her feet up on the coffee table, an iced tea in her hand and a guilty look on her face when I stand in front of her.

"I'm guessing you've spoken to your mother." She goes to reach forward so she can place her glass on the table but her huge stomach makes it a struggle. Despite being mad at her, I take it from her hands and do it for her, then resting my ass on the surface beside it I wait for her explanation.

"What were you thinking? Do you know how dangerous it could be?"

"I was thinking that all this hiding has to come to an end. You can offer him something he wants, he's always used me for power before."

I scrub my hand over my face and pray to a higher power for strength, this girl has no idea how complicated all this is. "Matteo, make an alliance, it's the only way for us to have a normal life."

"You hate my mom." I shake my head, ignoring what she's

asking of me, and wondering when the two of them conspired their little plan.

"Correction, your mother hates *me*. But she also believes we met in the same way we will tell my father we did. She agrees that an alliance is the only way forward." She smiles, as she slouches back on the couch, and I take a seat beside her, rolling up the tee she's wearing to reveal her stomach. It seems weird seeing her with so many clothes on here, she's practically lived in a bikini while we've been on the island. I rub my hand in big circles that span over her huge, swollen belly and focus on what's important.

Aria has no idea how deep her father's hatred for me is, he wanted me dead, and I have no doubt that his failure has made him any less determined to get the job done. Maybe seeing that I make his daughter happy will change his mind, but there's nothing in this world that will have me forgiving him for what I lost as a result of his efforts.

"I don't want you to worry about any of this. I just want you to focus on resting."

I'm mad at her, crazy fucking mad in fact, but I can't let that show. Everything has been going so smoothly with this pregnancy, up till now. I won't fail at the final hurdle.

"So, we're going to the party?" Aria bites her lip to try to hold off her smile.

"We're going to the party, But, you are going to be at my side all night. I won't let you out of my sight."

"That's a promise I can make." She smiles before she kisses me.

CHAPTER THIRTY-ONE

ARIA

"Mrs Romano, what a nice surprise." I somehow manage to scramble up off my back and onto my knees when Matteo's mom waltzes unexpectedly into the living room.

"What on earth are you doing?" She studies the yoga mat I was laid on, with a snarl on her lips.

"Oh, this? It's just a little yoga. It will, apparently, help with the birthing side of things, though I'm not sure what aids having to push a six-pound baby out of your..." I stop myself from rambling when the disgust on her face tells me I'm oversharing.

"Drugs, dear." She clears her throat before lighting up a cigarette, and despite me knowing that Matteo would be mad at her for it, I keep my mouth shut. We may have agreed that her party tomorrow night is a good idea, but the woman still detests me.

"Matteo has a few meetings he had to attend, is there something I can help you with?" I use the armchair to help me struggle back onto my feet. I'm so big these days that even doing the minimalist tasks feel like a huge effort. I can't even imagine our baby having three weeks of growing time left.

Vivian shows no sympathy in my discomfort, as I blow out a breath and waddle my way over to the couch.

"I came to finalize your outfit for tomorrow night. My friend is a designer, we've been talking over a few options and she'll be here in about half an hour with what she's done. She can make any adjustments needed." Her eyes widen when they look down at my stomach, making me very aware of the fact I'm only wearing shorts and a sports bra. I wasn't exactly expecting guests.

"Wait, you've organized what I'm wearing?" I check that I'm hearing her right.

"Darling, you are about to step out into society as Matteo Romano's wife. You can't just wear any old thing." Her laugh is condescending and makes me want to grip her over-bleached hair in my fist and rip it from her scalp.

"I'm much more focused on being comfortable these days," I inform her, just about managing to keep my cool. The idea of wearing anything other than stretch pants, or Matteo's sweats, makes me want to cry.

"It's one night, Aria, I'm sure you can make an effort. For the family." She throws one of her fake smiles at me.

"Ouch," I wince when the baby takes a sharp jab at my ribs, and Vivian responds by turning up her nose and looking in the other direction.

"Don't worry it's just a kick," I tell her sarcastically.

"Good, we don't want you doing anything stupid like going into labor, early. This party has taken a lot of organization in a very small amount of time."

"You could feel him if you want to. He's really active." Maybe feeling her grandson kick inside me will help form some kind of bond between us. I can't believe anyone would be so intentionally cold.

"No, thank you." She shakes her head and clicks her finger

for Anita to come and when she arrives in the lounge she bows her head and starts fumbling with her apron.

"Mrs Romano, we weren't–"

"Expecting me? I know. I like to make my visits spontaneous," Vivian interrupts her. "Be a dear and get me a dirty Martini. Anna, here, will have an iced water." Anita nods her head and scurries off, while Matteo's mother decides to light her second cigarette.

"I never wanted children, you know." She surprises me when she's finished studying my frame thoughtfully.

"To Angelo, it was my sole purpose. I was the privileged one who got to give him his heir," She laughs spitefully.

"I love Matteo," I point out.

"I did my duty, and you are doing yours." She shrugs as if my words don't matter.

"And what's your duty, now?" I ask, wondering how this woman will fit into the life me and Matteo want to make.

"To make sure my son doesn't fuck everything up that he has inherited. It's not just his father's name and legacy that is at stake. My family's fortune was the reasoning behind mine and Angelo's arranged marriage. It was done to protect both our families' power."

"And, now?" I frown back at her.

"And now, I am the richest woman this side of the state, and my son will inherit that once I'm gone. Your father knows this, Aria, the Romano name has far surpassed his. He will bend to whatever Matteo demands."

"Is this you reassuring me that everything's going to work out?" I question if the cold bitch may have thawed a little.

"This is me telling you that it has to. My son will kill your father before he lets him take you away from him. You might want to be prepared for that." She steps closer to me and leans into my ear.

"To be a Romano wife, you have to be able to forgive. Popping out heirs is the easy part," she whispers.

"Mother." Matteo steps through the door, right on cue. Immediately snatching the cigarette from his mother's fingers and stubbing it out in the nearest plant pot.

"I've told you about making unannounced visits," he warns.

"And I've chosen to ignore you," she smiles, taking the Martini from the tray Anita has returned with.

"I'm here to get Aria ready for the party tomorrow night." Vivian proves that her calling me by the wrong name is intentional. "Menika is on her way over. You remember Menika, don't you darling? There was a time when the two of you were close, was there not?" She looks at me over her shoulder and smiles, while Matteo keeps a deadly stern look on his face. The awkward silence is disrupted by the crackle of Demitri's radio when the guard's voice fills the room as he announces the arrival of a guest.

"Let her in," Demitri confirms, after receiving a nod from Matteo. Vivian looks across to me with a smug smile as she balances her ass on the arm of the couch and smooths out the pencil skirt, she's wearing.

"This will be fun."

Menika arrives in the living room after being dragged through all the security checks Demitri has put in place. I notice the dreamy look on her face when she spots Matteo and I hate her already. She is, of course, perfectly pretty, with long, blonde hair that seems to have a natural flow, and a set of slender legs that she's clearly not ashamed to show off.

"Menika." Matteo nods his head at her curtly, and she looks disappointed when he offers her his hand to shake.

"Very formal these days, Matteo. No kisses?"

"I make a habit of only putting my mouth on my wife." He moves to stand beside me, wrapping his arm around my hip and dragging me closer.

"I'm sure Mother, here, shared our happy news with you." He strokes his free hand over my bulging stomach while I lift my ring-fingered hand and show her my big, shiny diamond and wedding band. Pregnancy hormones are a real thing. They heighten all your emotions and it seems jealousy isn't an exception.

"She did, congratulations." Menika fakes a smile at us both.

"I'm afraid your time has been wasted, Aria already has the dress she will be wearing to tomorrow's party," he informs them, taking me by surprise, at the same time.

"Is there any chance of me actually choosing for myself what I wear?" I interrupt.

"I thought you might like to wear the dress you wore to our wedding. You looked so beautiful that day, I think all Mother's guests should witness it for themselves."

"Oh, please, Matteo, that dress was off the rack, and very informal. This party is–"

"I like that idea," I interrupt Vivian, and smile up at Matteo. The dress has sentimental value, and I don't want to wear something Menika has designed. There is, however, a slight problem. "I've gotten a lot bigger since then. I don't know if it would still fit." I chew at my bottom lip and feel my cheeks flush pink.

"Then we shall go try it, now. If it doesn't fit, we'll figure something out." Matteo takes my hand and starts leading me toward the hall.

"You can leave now," he calls back to his mother and Menika.

"Matteo, that was rude," I whisper at him, as we start taking the stairs to our room. "I'm sure your mom was only trying to help."

"She was being controlling," he points out, supporting me as I struggle up the steps. And all I can do is laugh at him and shake my head

Once we're inside our room, he closes the door and heads straight for the wardrobe to take out the white dress, I married him in. His mother is right, it *is* understated, but it was comfortable and has happy memories attached to it.

"You want me to try it on, now?" I feel that heat flush my skin, again. My body has changed so dramatically these past few months, it's hard not to be a little conscious.

"Yes, I want you to try it on, now." He slides it off the hanger and moves closer to me.

"Like I said, I've grown a lot since I last wore it." I look down at myself and sigh.

"Why are you looking at yourself like that?" he questions, in the same harsh tone that he talks to his guards in.

"Like what?"

"Like you're ashamed of your body. Aria you're–."

"Did you fuck her?" I interrupt, raising my eyes back up to focus on his, and waiting patiently for his answer.

"Yes. Some time ago," he gives it to me straight. "I've fucked a lot of women, Aria." His answer makes the threat of tears sting my eyes.

"Well, that makes me feel better." I huff a sarcastic laugh, and try not to look at my huge overstretched stomach, while I think about the skinny, blonde bitch he fucked *some time ago* who's downstairs, right now.

Snatching the dress from his hands, I narrow my eyes at him, as I wriggle into it, stretching it over my bump and just about managing to make it fit. It's tight, and my stomach has never looked bigger, but I'm in the damn thing.

"As I was saying..." Matteo positions himself behind me, slowly walking me over to the full-length mirror, that's hung beside the bathroom door, and sliding his hands around my middle.

"...I've fucked a lot of women, but I've only ever been in love with one." He looks at me through our reflection, as he places a kiss on my cheek, and the sincerity in his eyes makes it really hard not to smile back at him. Especially, when I realize I may have overreacted a little.

Matteo never invited that woman to be in our house. It was his mother, who seems intent on making me feel uncomfortable.

"I'm sorry, I'm just feeling a little self-conscious..." I hold out my hands and look down at my ever-growing body. "I'm not exactly how I used to be, am I?" I blink back tears.

"You're kidding, right?" Matteo laughs at me. "Aria, do you have *any* idea how utterly obsessed I am with your body, right now?" His hand rubs a huge circle over my protruding belly. "I think this is beyond fucking sexy. You have a part of me inside you. You're growing us a child. And looking insanely fucking *hot* in the process. I wanted you to wear this dress because I knew it would be tight. I knew it would make this huge, beautiful bump stand out, and I want every single person in that room, tomorrow, to see what I did to you. I want them to know that you're mine and that our son grows big and healthy. And Aria... you better get used to looking this kind of beautiful, because I intend to have you big and round with plenty more Romano babies."

Now, there's nothing I can do to stop the tearful little giggle that comes out, and when Matteo spins me around and kisses me hard on my lips, his hand slips under my dress and leaves me with no doubt that he just meant everything he said.

CHAPTER THIRTY-TWO

MATTEO

I can't believe Aria would doubt how beautiful she looks right now, and I could curse my mother and her stupid, designer friend for coming here today.

I've been edgy enough due to the loose ends I had to tie up this morning, that dragged me away from her. And after I convinced Aria that her wedding dress will be the perfect thing for her to wear to Mom's party, I fuck her in it before we take a bath together. I'm doing all I can to keep her mind off tomorrow night, even if it was her own stupid idea. We have dinner on the patio, and watch some crap on TV, that she's recently become addicted to. Now, it's time for me to take my wife to bed and worship her.

"Come on." I hold out my hand to help drag her off the couch, placing my other hand under her stomach, to support it, as she stands. She's really starting to struggle with how heavy it's gotten. Dr Fabier gave her a scan the day after we got back from the island, and he estimates the baby is almost six pounds, already. There's plenty more time for him to grow before Aria's due date, and she's only going to get bigger. The thought of her swelling, even rounder, makes me constantly fucking hard when I'm around her.

She waddles up the stairs with me and when we get to our room, as soon as the door is closed, I snatch her hips and drag her closer.

"I much preferred being on the island. You hide yourself away far too much here." I slide the vest top, she's wearing, up over her huge, full tits so I can squeeze one in my hand. Aria got embarrassed the other night when I made them leak, but I fucking loved it, so much so, that I had to taste it or myself.

"Matteo!" she warns, clearly scared of it happening again, and since I want tonight to be for her pleasure only, I manage to refrain.

"Are you wet for me?" I slip my fingers under her bump and into her panties and when she instantly soaks them, it makes me growl like a starving wolf. I should be going easy on her. I've read that sex can induce labor, but Fabier has assured me that that only happens in cases where the baby is ready to come. Since we have another three weeks before that happens, I intend to give my wife exactly what she needs.

"We'll probably have to do it with me on all fours again. I'm far too big for you to go on top." She blushes adorably, even if it does make me mad that she's hung up on her growing body.

"I have a better idea." I lead her over to the bed, pushing off my sweatpants and sitting on the mattress. I watch her confused face as I pull my t-shirt over my head and lay myself back against the headboard. "I want you on top. I want to watch you take my cock, while this big, beautiful bump bounces in front of me."

"*Matteo.*" Aria flushes pink again, and when I sit back up and drag her closer, so she's standing beside the bed, I rub my palm over her tightly-stretched skin and make soft kisses across it.

"Don't you want to take full control of my cock? Decide for yourself exactly how you get it? Hard or fast, gentle, or slow?" I tease her pussy with my finger as I look up at her over the swell of her tummy.

She proves she sees the incentive in my request when she tosses off her bra and carefully climbs onto the bed, and when I rest back again she takes her position, straddling my lap. I admire the view of her as she reaches under her belly and takes me in her hand, and I'm more than happy to assist, as she lines me up with her entrance and slowly sits herself on my steel-hard cock. The warmth of her pussy, and the way it sucks around me, has me clutching at her thighs and moaning.

"That's fucking perfect," I tell her, letting her set the pace, as she takes me deep and slow, with each roll of her hips.

"It feels good like this," she confesses, reaching her arms behind her and gripping at my ankles, it pushes her stomach out even more, and I cradle both sides of it in my hands while she drenches my cock and her pussy tightens around me.

"I'm gonna come like this," she announces, in that cute, helpless voice Lowering one of my hands, I use my thumb and strum her clit to help her get there a little faster.

The noises she makes when she comes for me has me close to coming, myself, but I manage to hold back. My wife deserves to come more than once. She throws back her head and screams my name, as she rides out her pleasure, then when she's finished I decide it's time for me to take control.

I grab at her hips lifting her slightly so I can fuck her hard and fast, straight into another orgasm. She's barely had time to recover, and this time, instead of reaching back, she reaches forward, clutching the headboard as I thrust into her from underneath and make her come all over my cock, again. I allow myself to come too, forcing her down onto my cock one last time, and holding her still so I can fill her pussy to the brim.

"You good" I stroke her stomach, while I get my breath back and when I look up and see her nodding at me, I smile.

"Aria, never doubt how fucking incredible you are again." I grab her throat and drag her down onto my lips.

CHAPTER THIRTY-THREE

ARIA

"You look incredible," Matteo tells me when I meet him at the bottom of the staircase. I've gripped my hair up the same way Grena did for our wedding and once again squeezed myself into my wedding dress. Matteo looks hot as sin in his tuxedo, and now there is nothing left to do, other than leave.

"You don't scrub up too bad yourself." I dust off his shoulder before he grabs my hips and pulls me close.

"Are you ready to face the world, Mrs Romano?" He presses his forehead against mine, making my stomach flip when I'm reminded that tonight, everything will become real again. No more living in Matteo's protective bubble, no more secrets. I have to have the faith that this will go well.

"I'm ready." I drop my hand into his and let him lead me out the door, toward the car, where Demitri is getting into the front passenger seat. There are three other cars waiting to escort us. One in front of the car we're taking and two behind it. Everything seems like a military mission as his guards fill them.

"Is all this really necessary?" I ask, accepting Matteo's help as I lower myself into the backseat of the car.

"I'm not taking any risks." Matteo puts on a brave smile, as he leans across my body to fix my safety belt.

"Try not to worry." He places a kiss on my cheek before sitting back in his seat and clutching his hands together, tight. I can tell how wound up he is, by the white of his knuckles, and although I stand by my decision that what we're doing here is our safest option, even Vivian agrees that her impressive guest list will offer Matteo and me full protection. My father cares very much about his reputation, it's unlikely he would attempt anything in front of a crowd. And one thing I know I can rely on Vivian Romano for is her ability to draw the right crowd. I swear the people of L.A. fear her, just as much as they do her son.

We travel to Malibu and when our car pulls through the huge, black gates, and parks outside the mansion home that belongs to Matteo's mother, I'm not at all surprised by its elegance.

"Remember, stay close." Matteo kisses my cheek, again, before getting out of the car and reaching back in to help me out. When I notice the amount of security he has set up here too, I start feeling *really* nervous.

"Aria, darling." His mother greets us in the foyer with a warm, over-the-top welcome, and I look at Matteo in shock when she makes a big fuss and affectionately rubs my bump. "I'm so glad you made it." Tugging me in for a hug, she lowers her tone to a whisper. "He's not here yet," she confirms, pasting on her smile as she takes a glass of champagne from the waiter holding the tray. "Come, there are people I want you to meet." She links her arm into mine and leads me into her living room. Matteo stays close behind us. Refusing a drink when he's offered and remaining on edge. I try to stay relaxed, there are a lot more people here than I expected and it's been a long time since I've had to be social. Vivian's home reminds me of a museum, with its tall ceilings, random sculptures, and the elaborate art that decorates her walls. Anyone can see that she loves entertaining, and I do my best to smile and nod as she introduces me to some of her guests. Despite being on his guard, Matteo is tentative to me, making sure one of the waiters gets me an iced water and keeping his hand wrapped tightly around mine. I can feel how clammy his palm is, and notice how his eyes constantly shift around the room. There are guards on every door, with more of them randomly placed around the room and when I notice Demitri pressing his hand over the earpiece he's wearing, the nod he gives Matteo tells me this is it. I'm starting to think this was a really bad idea, I feel sick, and my stomach is cramping like I need to use the bathroom.

"Aria Fucchini!" A voice I recognise calls out from behind us. Silencing all the chatty voices and the sound of the harp being played in the corner of the room.

Matteo's whole body tenses as we both turn around and face the man we've been avoiding for almost a year. My father looks different to how I remember, smaller somehow and much older. His eyes drop to my bulging stomach and stretch with shock and fury.

"Her name is no longer Fucchini...Aria is a Romano now," Matteo corrects him, showing no fear. He lifts up my hand to show him my wedding band, as evidence.

All his nerves seem to have vanished, he's as steady as a rock and I realize I'm seeing the version of Matteo Romano that the rest of the world gets, now.

"What is this?" My father starts striding toward us, and one of Matteo's guards immediately blocks his path.

"Get out of my way, that is my daughter!" he yells, pointing his finger over the guard's shoulder at me. "Aria, explain!"

My mouth moves to speak but no words come out. I can tell from the look on his face that he had no idea I would be here.

"Stevan, will you not congratulate us? Aria is soon to deliver you a healthy grandson." There's a sarcastic bite to Matteo's tone as he strokes his hand proudly over my bump, and my father says nothing, just glances at the crowd surrounding us, looking overwhelmed.

"Aria, it's been a while since I saw you." He manages to pull himself back together and pastes on a smile, "Perhaps you and I could talk in private."

Matteo places himself in front of me, protectively.

"I'd like a word with you myself, first," he tells him.

"Very well." My father nods his head, and when Matteo turns around to face me, the pure rage on his face makes me even more anxious.

"I'll make this right," he promises, kissing my forehead before he steps towards my father and stands down his guard.

"Follow me. I have somewhere private we can talk." I hear him utter to my father as he passes him, not looking back to check if he follows as he marches back through to the hall. My father shakes his head at me in disappointment before he turns around and follows after my husband.

"Well, I think that went rather well." Vivian smiles, toasting her glass before she continues talking to the couple she introduced me to, a few minutes ago. The air around me starts to feel tight, the walls feel like they're spinning and when I notice one of Matteo's guards standing watch by the patio doors, I head straight over to him.

"I need some air." I clasp at the necklace I'm wearing when it starts feeling like it's choking me, and he nods his head quickly, checking the coast is clear before he moves aside and lets me out.

He remains close and vigilant, no doubt on Matteo's orders and I make his job a little easier for him by taking a chair at the bistro table that's close to the door. I take in some deep breaths and try to stay calm, but the fact my father and husband hate each other and are currently in the same room doesn't make it easy. I hear the sound of heels clicking against the marble floor and when I look back toward the door I see Menika. She looks disgustingly beautiful, and skinny, in the long, glittery dress she's wearing.

"Are you okay, I saw you rush out?" She seems to be genuinely concerned, and I must be desperate for a distraction because I nod my head at Matteo's guard so he'll let her pass.

"Vivian explained the situation to me, I'm sure Matteo will smooth things over with your father, he's very good at negotiating," she assures me, pulling up a chair and sitting beside me. I doubt very much that Vivian has told her *everything* but I smile gratefully, anyway.

"And is this the part where you tell me that's not all he's good at?" I raise my eyebrows and slouch back in my chair, the baby's dropped much lower these past few days, and having him press against my pelvis is becoming really uncomfortable.

"Well, I won't deny it." She shrugs, and something about the face she pulls actually has me laughing.

"Look, what me and Matteo had wasn't special. I was a distraction for him at a time when he was really struggling," she admits, almost becoming human.

"When his father died?" I nod sadly, thinking back to the conversation I had with him on the beach. I can tell how affected Matteo is by his father's death, and the fact Matteo wants to do things so differently with our child proves that he's going to be a great father.

"No, when he lost Thalia and their baby." Menika's words

send my body into shock and when I look up at her in confusion, she immediately slams her hand over her mouth.

"What did you just say?" I check I've heard her right, sitting back up straight.

"Nothing, just forget it. I... I should get back to the party." She goes to stand up but I grab her arm and drag her back down.

"No, you will tell me what you just said," I order, my heart starting to thump wildly in my chest as the sick feeling in my gut grows stronger.

"I don't think I should. You should speak to Matteo. I'm sorry, I thought you knew." She looks really scared, and the fact she's not giving me answers infuriates me.

"I'm asking *you* to tell me." I act on high emotion and impulse when I clutch her throat in my hands and stare into her eyes.

"Don't you *dare* interfere," I tell Matteo's guard when I catch a glimpse of him moving toward me from the corner of my eye.

A cramp in the base of my stomach forces me to close my eyes and squeeze Menika's neck a little tighter, but it passes after a few seconds and I quickly get back to focusing on her.

"There was an accident about two years ago, Matteo lost his girlfriend and their unborn child." I release her from my grip so I can stand on my feet, resting my hand on the table while I try to get all my thoughts in check.

What I'm hearing can't be true. Matteo has never mentioned anything about a dead ex, or another baby. Just yesterday he told me I was the only woman he's ever loved.

"I'm taking over here. We need more men in the foyer....Aria." I look up when I hear my name and see Demitri racing toward me. The guard he just spoke to scurries away and when I look up at him I can tell straight away that something's wrong.

"Did you know about this?" I ask, clutching my stomach and reminding myself to stay calm. Though it's hard to do when I suddenly feel trapped in a web of lies.

"Aria, we have to leave." Demitri's voice sounds panicked as he grabs my elbow.

"I'm not going anywhere until you tell me if what she's saying is true." I rip my elbow out of his hands.

"What? What has she said to you?" He frowns at Menika impatiently, his eyes scanning the door he just walked through, like he's on edge.

"She told me that Matteo was expecting a child with another woman and that he lost them both." I narrow my eyes, daring him to try lying to me.

"Aria, we really have to leave. Matteo needs me to take you somewhere safe."

"Tell me!" I feel the tears building in my eyes as the betrayal sinks in.

"It's true, and I'll explain everything, but first you have to let me get you somewhere safe. Please." There's a desperation in his eyes that I've never seen before.

"What's happened?" In spite of my anger, I focus on what he's been trying to say, something must have gone wrong. And I see no signs of Matteo.

"Where's Matteo?" I start to panic. It doesn't matter that I'm hurting, or mad at him. I need him and he's not here. Worse still, there's a chance he could be in danger.

"Aria, we have to go, come on!" Demitri takes a firmer hold of me and starts dragging me around the side of the house into darkness, and when I look back at Menika she shakes her head at me, in confusion, before heading back inside.

"Demitri, you need to tell me what's happened. Where is

Matteo?" He remains silent as he leads me to a car that's parked out of view, behind Vivian Romano's huge garage.

"Matteo had an escape plan organized just in case something went wrong. This is the escape plan," he eventually tells me, opening the passenger door and leaving me no choice but to get inside.

CHAPTER THIRTY-FOUR

MATTEO

"Do you want to explain to me what the *fuck* is going on?" Stevan Fucchini sounds fuming. Despite all my own anger, I manage to remain calm when I close the door to my father's old office and take a seat behind his desk.

"I should kill you!" he snarls at me through his teeth, and I say nothing, just stare the evil bastard right in his eyes.

"But you won't. Innocent women and unborn babies are much more your style," I point out, waiting for him to show some form of reaction.

"What are you talking about, Matteo?" He shakes his head, impatiently. "We both know you marrying my daughter and knocking her up with the next Romano heir, is your version of a very distasteful joke. I've been out of my mind with worry. It's almost been a fucking year!"

"Don't give me bullshit, we both know your daughter is nothing to you. Just a pawn. You were going to marry her to the wrinkly, old bastard. You were going to sacrifice her chance of happiness for your own gain," I tell him, feeling all the rage, I'm trying to hold off, building stronger.

"Every father has to make arrangements for their daughter,

you know that. It's how our world works. Dennis wouldn't have lasted many more years. He had no heirs. When he died she would have inherited everything."

"And why would she need to? She is the daughter of the *great* Stevan Fucchini." I throw my hands in the air sarcastically, and when his eyes drop to the floor, I get the impression something isn't right.

"Not anymore." There's a disgruntled look on his face when he pulls his eyes back up to mine.

"What are you talking about?" I shake my head in confusion.

"I've lost it all," he mutters under his breath. "I made some judgment errors. I relied on the wrong people. For years now, I have been steering a sinking ship." He leaves his pride on the fucking table and suddenly looks completely different from the man who stormed in here, after me.

"That's not true, you've just invested in some big development. You came here because you knew where Aria was and you wanted to try and take her back."

"Matteo, I had no idea where my daughter was, I've spent a whole year trying to fucking find her. I've hired investigators, I even went to the *fucking law*." He shakes his head, helplessly. "I came here to invest the last of what I have, in something stable. I'm done working with deceitful men."

I can tell from the expression on his face that he's telling the truth. He looks tired, and a little broken.

"I may have nothing left to my name, Romano, but I won't forgive you for this."

"I'm not asking for your forgiveness. If there is any man in this room who will have to find the strength of forgiveness, it will be me," I remind him, thinking about the child I lost, and the innocent woman who didn't need to die.

"I don't know what the fuck you speak of, Matteo, but Aria

has *never* been a pawn in my game, she will not be one in yours." He seems to gain some strength back and when he points his finger at me over the desk, I laugh at him.

"I'm afraid this has gone way beyond a game, it's even gone beyond my hate for you." I drop the cocky smirk from my lips and get real with him. "I'm in love with your daughter. She belongs to me now, and I won't spend the rest of our lives looking over my shoulder and waiting for you to try and take her. Despite our differences, despite the hate I have for you, we will not leave this room until we have come up with a resolution that keeps her happy." I give it to him straight, fully aware that I'm going to have to swallow some pride of my own. My need for vengeance has transformed into a desperation for something else.

"Matteo, I never blamed you for the sins of your father. After he died I hoped me and you could form an alliance. That is why I accepted your mother's invitation this evening. I don't want to be your enemy."

"And attempting to kill me was your way of doing that?" I scoff another laugh at him and when I see that confusion on his face again, it makes me want to snap his fucking neck.

"I have no idea what you are talking about." He stares back at me blankly.

"The car you had blown up, that you expected me to be in…a woman who carried my child was in that car. Your fear of me, and the need to eliminate my threat killed them both." I feel all the tension gather in my fists as I clench them together.

"Matteo. Listen to me. I don't know where you heard that, but I can swear that I had nothing to do with it." Stevan is looking really fucking worried now, but beyond that, his confusion is still visible.

"I'll tell you exactly who told me that. Marco Laurent, the man who works for you, but answers to me. He has been living in your home for two years now." I wait for him to realize that any attempts of denial would be hopeless.

"I have never had a staff member called Marco Laurent." He shakes his head, and the niggle that's been scratching away at me since we entered this room makes me wonder if he's speaking the truth.

"Demitri had him enter your home after the accident. He's been our eyes and ears, ever since," I tell him again, starting to feel a little unnerved.

"Most of my staff were let go last year, due to my lack of finances. I have only kept a few employees, those who have been loyal to me over the years," he assures me. "And you have to believe me when I tell you, I made no attempt on your life. I may not be a good man but I am an honorable one. If I'd have wanted you dead I'd have looked you in the eye while I did it." There's a hint of threat in his tone, but I don't take it seriously. I know for a fact my men would have disarmed him at the door. He has nobody with him. He is no threat to me or Aria. What I'm more concerned about is who's lying to me, him or my best friend.

"I need to speak with Demitri." I stand up, forcing my hand through my hair in frustration as I stomp toward the door and rip it open. The two guards standing outside immediately turn to look at me.

"Where's Demitri?" I ask the one on my left.

"I'm not sure sir, last I heard through the radio, he was doing a perimeter check." I march past him back into the living room where the party is now in full swing. I scan my eyes around the room looking for Demitri, and in doing so, realize that there is no sign of Aria, either.

"I want to see my daughter." Stevan's voice comes from behind me, making me realize he's followed me out.

A horrid sense of unease creeps over my skin and I don't know what it is, but I sense something isn't right.

"Matteo." Menika rushes towards me when she sees me. "Are you okay?"

"Not now. I don't have time." I shove her out my way and head toward the guard I have standing at the patio doors.

"Matteo!" The blonde bitch doesn't get the hint.

"I'm sorry, I thought she knew. I was trying to reassure her that I was no threat and it just came out." I slowly turn around when I hear what she just said. The quiver in her voice and the way her eyes fill up with tears suggests she's afraid.

"What, Menika? What came out? Where is Aria?" I grab her shoulders in my hands and squeeze them in frustration.

"Demitri took her, he said there was something wrong." She looks back at me confused, and I instantly drop her from my grip and rush toward my guard, grabbing him by the lapels of his suit and shoving him into the wall.

"Where is Demitri?" I ask, just about ready to murder someone.

"I don't know, he took over from me about ten minutes ago. Told me more staff were needed in the foyer. I got there and the boys said they had it covered so I came back. Demitri was with her when I left, boss. I wouldn't have let her out of my sight if he wasn't."

"Get him on the fucking radio!" I yell, trying my best not to panic. There will be a logical reason for this.

"What's happening? Where is my daughter?" Stevan asks, almost looking as angry as I am.

I breathe myself calm and try to think straight. Maybe Aria needed to use the bathroom, she's always needing the bathroom these days. I'll bet he's taken her upstairs because the one in the hall was being used.

"That was Niko, boss." My guard takes his hand away from his earpiece,

"He said Demitri went out the front gate ten minutes ago, with Miss Aria in the passenger seat." He swallows thickly and drops his eyes to the ground. "He told them it was on your order."

The walls suddenly feel like they're collapsing in on me, and I swear my legs are gonna give in. I'm standing in a room full of people who fear and respect me and I can't show how scared I have just become.

"Matteo..." Stevan looks at me, shaking his head in confusion.

"I gave no such order," I tell him weakly.

CHAPTER THIRTY-FIVE

ARIA

"This is where Matteo told you to bring me?" I look at the abandoned cabin that Demitri stops the car in front of. It doesn't exactly scream 'Matteo Romano' vibes, which is probably why he's chosen it as his safe place. I'm just happy the journey is over, we had to go off-road to get here, and it was a very uncomfortable, bumpy ride. My stomach is churning like I'm gonna throw up.

"This is it," Demitri confirms, getting out of the car. He opens the back door and grabs the holdall that's resting on the back seat.

"I hope Matteo packed some comfortable clothes in there." I smile at him over my shoulder, knowing that Matteo is always attentive to detail. He would have thought this plan through. I have to trust it. Opening my own door, I manage to hoist myself out of the car; just as I'm about to follow Demitri to the door, another pain shoots across my stomach, catching me off guard. I rest one hand on the car roof and rub the side of my tummy with the other until it passes. I felt a few similar twinges on the way here, but that one felt much stronger.

"You okay?" Demitri turns around to ask before he opens the door.

"Yeah, I'm good, it's just been an eventful night." I fake him a smile and follow him inside. I can tell something is wrong. Demitri is even more tense than usual. The last thing I want to do is stress him. He's refusing to tell me what happened back at the party, and I'm assuming that's on Matteo's orders too. I've read that you can get practice contractions around this stage of pregnancy and everything else, up to now, has been pretty textbook.

I step through the door, surprised when I see how empty the place is. There's an old rusty bed, with no mattress, against the back wall and a stool in the corner of the room. The small kitchen worktop is covered in dust and I feel it stick to the back of my throat when Demitri slams his holdall on the surface and disturbs it.

"When was the last time anyone came here?" I ask, running my finger through the dust.

"Sorry, it's not up to standard, *Princess*." Demitri bolts the door, and takes a seat on the stool, scrubbing his hand over his face and shaking his head.

"Demitri, I know this is a bad time, but I really need to know what happened back there. And what the hell was Menika talking about? Am I supposed to be some kind of replacement? Is that the reason he took me?" I have so many questions, and I'm starting to feel really fucking scared.

"Just... stop talking!" Demitri shocks me when he raises his voice at me, I'm not used to seeing him like this. He's always so put-together and controlled, but now, he seems irate and a little manic.

"Sit down." He gestures his head toward the corner of the room.

"I'd rather stand," I tell him, rubbing the ache in the base of my spine and starting to feel really uneasy about this whole situation.

"*Will you just do as your fucking told?*" My breath jams in my throat when he pulls a gun out from the inside of his jacket and points it at me.

"Okay." I hold up my trembling hands, defensively, as I carefully lower myself onto the floor in the opposite corner to the one he's sitting in.

"What's up, Demitri?" I ask, trying to keep my voice calm as I realize me and my baby are in danger.

"It wasn't supposed to be them. That was *Matteo's* fucking car," he tells me. "*He* put her in it. She died because of *him*. Not me." He shakes his head.

I have no idea what I'm dealing with here, but I do my best to sound understanding.

"Does Matteo know we're here?" I ask, praying to God that he does.

"No, Aria. Matteo has no idea you're here." His mood switches again when he laughs at me, mockingly. My body tenses when another pain ripples through me. This time I can't hide it, my face screws up as my stomach tightens and this one seems to last much longer than the one I had outside.

"Demitri, I think I need to see a doctor. I've started having contractions. The baby could be on its way." I tell him, hoping I can reason with him.

"Do you really expect me to believe that?" he laughs, again. "Your little games may have worked on Matteo but they won't work on me." He shakes his head.

"Demitri, I'm being serious, they've been happening since we left the party." A whole new type of panic forms in my chest when it sinks in that I could actually be in labor and Matteo has no idea where I am.

"I told him not to take you. But Matteo will never be told. It always has to be *his* way." Demitri starts pacing the floor in front of me.

"You know, before he died, Angelo Romano offered my father his entire empire. He thought Matteo was too young to take over, that he still had much to learn. All my father had to do was end his life for him. That was just like Angelo, everything was a game, even his own death."

"I know what happened, Matteo told me," I assure him. "It was a cruel game to play, it was too much to ask of Matteo, and of your father."

"He could have asked me, I would have done it." Demitri leans down so his nose is almost touching mine. "It *should* have been me," he whispers. His chest rises and falls rapidly as he works himself up. "Angelo knew. He pretended he didn't, to me, but *he* knew." Demitri shakes his head.

"Who knew?" I try to keep him talking, hoping I can somehow calm him down and find a way out of this.

"Angelo. He knew he was my father. That I am the true heir to all of this." He stretches out his arms.

"You think you're Matteo's brother?" I ask in shock.

"Not just his brother, his *older* brother." He points out, standing up and moving away from me. He grips the kitchen counter so tight, his knuckles turn white.

"My mother got pregnant with me, three months before Vivian did. Angelo was never going to upset Vivian's family, he needed them. He had an heir on the way, so he had no reason to claim the child of one of his servants," he explains, his voice so angry that it shakes.

"This place is where I was born, on that rusty bed where my mother thought she would die from the pain she was in. This is what he offered my mother when he found out she carried his child. A shack, hidden away in the forest. Before she died she told me the truth. She told me that after I was born she carried me to the main house and presented me to him. By then everyone was awaiting the arrival of Vivian's child. I was a complication he couldn't risk. He needed to control the situation, so he had one of his men marry my mother and claim me as his own."

"That was wrong of him." I show Demitri some empathy, hoping to buy some time, enough time for Matteo to find us.

"My father was his protector, his advisor and everything that *I* am to Matteo. He offered him all this on his deathbed because he knew it should have been mine."

I don't have any words, Demitri's state of mind is too fragile and I have far too much at stake.

"I was trying to make things right, I never meant for them to die. Matteo was supposed to be in that fucking car," he repeats; I scream uncontrollably when he punches his fist hard into the wood surface, and a contraction squeezes my belly so tight, it takes my breath away.

"Demitri, the baby's definitely coming. I need to get to a doctor." I tell him, breathing steadily like the woman demonstrated on the YouTube video Matteo made us watch.

"I can't do that, Aria. See, tonight wasn't supposed to go down the way it did. Your father was not supposed to come. He must be crazy." Demitri chuckles. "I tried to play things the opposite way this time. Matteo always goes against my advice. He's hot-headed, he strikes before he thinks and I was certain that your father would be too fucking afraid to come. But, right now, they'll be making negotiations over your future. Matteo is going to learn that I lied to him about everything. He's going to know that it was me that put that fucking bomb in his trunk."

My body starts to shake uncontrollably, I don't know if it's the shock of what's happening to my body or from fear, but I can feel myself losing all my calm.

"Demitri, listen to me. My baby is coming now. I *need* a doctor."

"That's what they call poetic justice, Aria. It's proof that I'm right."

"What are you talking about?" I feel my panic heighten when he zips open the holdall that he brought with him.

"You and Matteo are not the only ones who have been doing their research." Slowly he starts to unpack the bag and when I see the surgical knife and the cord clamps he carefully places on the kitchen surface, it takes all my strength not to scream.

"Your child may not be full term but it's viable." Keeping the gun in his hand he comes back toward me and strokes the barrel across my stomach.

"The fact you may have gone into labor yourself, is good for you, Aria. If you can deliver your son naturally, you may be able to survive. I didn't want to have to cut you open," he tells me, calmly. I feel tears filling my eyes and keep reminding myself to breathe, but with the discomfort of my body and panic in my chest, it feels impossible.

"We'll find out tonight how much your child really means to Matteo because once I have him, there will be only one way for Matteo to get him back."

I splay my hands against the wall to help me get back on my feet. I will not sit back and let him threaten my child. I have to get us out of here.

"What are you doing? Sit back down." He thunders back toward me, wrapping his hand around my neck and slamming me hard against the wall.

"Demitri, I want us to talk calmly about this. You don't want to hurt me *or* my baby. I know that. You just said yourself, you told Matteo not to take me, you were protecting me before we even met." I wipe the tears from my eyes and smile at him.

"I need you to get us to a hospital or something bad could happen to the baby." I feel another pain start to build and automatically reach for his hand, squeezing tight and making a noise that doesn't even sound like it comes from me. I grimace as the pain takes over all my senses, and when I look up at Demitri I beg him with my eyes for help. What I see looking back at me is pure evil.

"I'm not your hero, Princess." He slams the handle of the gun into the back of my neck, making me dizzy, and when I crash onto the wooden floor, everything turns black.

CHAPTER THIRTY-SIX

MATTEO

"What the fuck is going on?" Aria's father follows me as I burst through my front door and call out her name. I can't bear not knowing where she is, it's driving me crazy. The whole car journey here, I've thought about where he might have taken her, and I've come up with nothing.

"*Matteo!*" Stevan places his hand on my shoulder to stop me and I swing round to face him, raising my fist to punch his face. I drop it when I see how worried he looks.

"I have no idea what the fuck's going on," I admit, shaking my head weakly and letting myself drop to sit on the staircase. "Demitri is my best friend, he wouldn't hurt her. He knows how much I love her." I tell him what I've been telling myself, ever since I left Mother's place. Even though I'm not entirely convinced of it. "I never gave that order," I say my thoughts out loud again, shaking my head and having no idea what to do next. If they aren't here, they could be anywhere.

"Matteo, think. Is there anywhere he could have gone, any reason why he'd want to hurt her?"

"If there was, do you think I'd be *fuckin'* sitting here?" I get back on my feet.

"Calm down." He holds his hand up in front of me. "I want to find her just as much as you do."

"What's happened?" Anita calls out from the top of the stairs, then when she sees how mad I am, she ties up her dressing gown as she rushes down them.

"Demitri left the party with Aria, he told the guards I ordered it, when I didn't and now, I have no idea where they are. There *has* to be an explanation, he has no reason to hurt her," I explain, pacing the floor and trying to come up with an explanation. Maybe, he got a tip-off and acted on it before having a chance to speak to me. Demitri always thinks ahead.

Anita closes her eyes, and I can tell from the look on her face that she knows something.

"What?" I stand in front of her. "*Tell me!*" I growl, as she looks up at me awkwardly.

"There's something I think you should know. You need to speak to Gino."

"I haven't got time to speak to fuckin' Gino, Anita. Tell me what I need to know, right now."

Gino retired to Italy after my father died, no one hears from him anymore. The man doesn't even bother with his own son, these days.

"There is a chance that Demitri is your brother," Anita admits, wrapping her dressing gown tighter around her body.

"*What the fuck did you just say?*" I stare back at her, blankly.

"Your father used this house, more often than his Malibu home, before you were born, you know he liked his own space." She drives me to the brink of insanity with more beating around the bush.

"Maria was a maid here, there was a closeness between them." She lowers her head as if time isn't of the fucking essence here and when I grab her and shake her, she quickly starts talking again.

"She kept the pregnancy a secret for as long as she could, and by the time she started to show, your mother had already announced the news that you were on the way. You were the legitimate heir of the family. But Demitri was the son, who was born first."

"Fuck!" I drop the old woman from my grip as I take in what she just told me.

"He loves you like a brother, Matteo, he wouldn't hurt Aria, not when he knows how precious she is to you," she assures me.

"Are you sure about that, Anita? Because Stevan here didn't know anything about that bomb that was put in my car." I question her judgment and when she looks to Stevan for confirmation, he nods his head back at her.

"You think that was Demitri?" Her hand trembles as it covers her mouth.

"He thinks he has the right to the power of this family, and power makes a man capable of anything. Did Gino know?"

"Your father was the one who ordered Gino to marry Maria, it was a security measure to ensure she never spoke out. Can you imagine the scandal if it did? Your mother, and her family, would have been furious, they were responsible for a lot of your father's power. They could have snatched it away at any time."

"And you never thought to tell me this?" I can feel my chest getting tighter when I realize this explanation resolves nothing, Aria is still out there somewhere and I don't know where.

"I've watched your friendship grow, I didn't ever think he'd hurt you. Up to now, he has shown you nothing but loyalty. I just thought it was a buried secret."

"Would Gino know where he would have taken her?" I ask,

desperately. I'm as sure, as I can be that, Aria is in danger now, and I need to find her.

"No. But I might," Anita assures me. "Gino didn't marry Maria until after Demitri was born, up until then she was given a place by your father, somewhere where she wouldn't be seen. Your father trusted no one. As soon as Maria started to show, he moved her out of the staff quarters and into a cabin on the grounds, where he would visit her. He made her false promises about what would happen when the child was born. She was alone when she gave birth to Demitri. He wasn't breathing when he came out and she revived him by herself. I was the only other person who knew about the child and that was because I was her best friend. Demitri knew that me and Maria used to be close. We spoke about his mother often."

"How is this helping us figure out where Aria is?" I'm feeling completely helpless, I'm so used to having control, now it's been taken away I'm a mess.

"About a week ago Demitri asked me to show him the cabin where he was born. I should have noticed that it was strange. Maria must have told him the truth before she died."

"You think he has Aria at that cabin?" I check.

"I think it would be a good place to start looking." She smiles at me, sadly.

"You have to show me where this cabin is." I take her arm and start dragging her toward the door. The grounds surrounding my home span for miles. I've run through the woods for years and I've never seen a cabin among them.

"We'll find her, Mr Romano," Anita assures me, rushing us out the door in her night clothes and slippers.

"I'm coming with you." Stevan follows after us. I stop and turn around to look at him.

"Can I trust you?" I ask.

"Matteo, your cunt of a friend has my daughter. As long as

your ambition is to make her safe, you can trust me." I hate that all I have to go on is his word and my gut instinct.

Taking a leap of faith, I hold my hand out to my driver who's standing by the door waiting for instruction.

"Give me your gun," I order, and when he places it in my hand, I clutch it by its barrel and offer it out to Aria's father. He won't be armed. My security checked everybody who entered my mother's home tonight, especially him.

"If you've got any thoughts in your head of turning that on me, then you better hope you're a good shot," I warn, before turning back around and heading out to get my wife.

CHAPTER THIRTY-SEVEN

ARIA

I wake up to crushing pain. It's not just in my stomach anymore, it rattles the bones of my entire body. I touch my hand between my legs and when I feel how wet the floor beneath me is, I know I'm in real trouble.

I look around the room hoping he's not here anymore, if he isn't I can take my chance and try to escape, in between the contractions I'm having. Though there doesn't seem much hope of that when I see him from the corner of my eye and feel another pain starting to build, already.

"Demitri!" I clutch my belly, shifting myself so my back is against the wall. I tense my body when another contraction paralyzes me.

"*Please.*" I've forgotten all the different ways to breathe, all I can think about now, are the things Dr Fabier told me could go wrong if I were to deliver without medical help.

"Please, Demitri. I need a hospital."

"I told you, Aria, my mother gave birth to me in this cabin. The heir to all the Romano fortune, and reputation, was pushed into the world from a dirty mattress on a rusty bed. I think it's fitting that your son comes into the world the same way." He chuckles to himself.

"Let's just get me safe. It's not too late. Matteo will forgive you, he loves you." I sob, because I know I'm going to end up having this baby here, with this unstable bastard.

"You think I want his forgiveness?" Demitri laughs even more hysterically. "Aria, I *want* his destruction. When your son is born, I will take him. Matteo will never find him, the only way he will get him back is to admit that everything is mine. He will have to stand down and give me the power or I will kill his son."

"*Fuck!*" I curse when another contraction punishes my body, the pressure between my legs is becoming unbearable, I feel an overwhelming urge to push but I know I can't. I can't deliver my son here, straight into the arms of a monster.

"Does it hurt?" The smug son of a bitch crouches down in front of me. I don't answer him, just stare into his eyes and let the hate I feel for him distract me from the pain I'm in.

"It's a shame the seed you filled your belly with wasn't mine, you could have had yourself a real little prince." He strokes his hand over my clenched, tight stomach, and I wish I had the energy to shove it away. Right now, I feel like I'm in too much pain to even keep my eyes open.

Light from outside shines through the cabin window and I wonder if it's daylight and we've been here all night. My chest sags with relief when I hear the heavy pounding on the door and Matteo screams my name.

Demitri stands up and grips his gun tighter in his hand. I scream when he snatches my hair and uses it to drag me across the floor, away from the door that rattles as Matteo tries to break it down.

It crashes open, and the fear I see on Matteo's face tells me everything I need to know. I focus on the pain that feels like it's splitting me in two, rather than the hard metal I can feel pressing into the top of my skull.

"Demitri, put the gun down." Matteo shocks me when he reaches down to the floor and lays his own gun flat. "You don't want to hurt her, to get to me."

"See, that's where you're wrong Matteo. I've come to learn that, me hurting her, is the only thing that *will* get to you." Demitri sounds so casual, and when I notice my father step in slowly behind Matteo, he looks just as fearful.

"The baby's coming," I whimper, throwing my head back and growling deeply when I can't hold off the resistance to push, any longer.

"I have to push."

"It's okay, Princess. I'm here now." Matteo's petrified, but he's doing his best to hide it from me.

"Demitri, your issue is with me, not with her. I have Anita outside, let me call her in here so she can help."

"What I want, is you dead. It was never meant to be Thalia, that day." I hear the shake in Demitri's voice, and when the pain I'm in becomes too much to bear, I decide I have to fight for the son I'm about to push into this world.

Twisting my head, I take the risk of a bullet when I sink my teeth deep into Demitri's leg. Matteo uses the distraction to dive onto him, struggling with him on the ground and smashing the hand, he's gripping the gun with, on the floor. I quickly scurry out of the way, placing myself back in the corner of the room so I can finally give in to my body's demands.

"Help her!" My father calls out, and Anita rushes through the door.

It's a relief to see her, but my relief is short-lived when the gun goes off with an ear-splitting bang.

CHAPTER THIRTY-EIGHT

MATTEO

Seeing him holding a gun to her head was enough to make my heart stop beating, and when Aria fought back, I knew her distraction would be my only chance. Demitri is bigger than me, he always has been. But I have the fight of a thousand armies inside me, as I attack him. The grip he has on the gun is too tight, it doesn't matter how many times I slam his hand into the ground, he's not giving it up; so I keep his wrist pinned while I smash my fist into his head, over and over, again. He manages to catch me with a left hook that sets me a little off guard, and when he lifts the gun, to point it at my face, I'm surprised when Aria's father comes in from my right and kicks Demitri's head like it's a football. The gun goes off, grazing through my shoulder instead of my skull; when I look up at the man who just saved my life, he nods his head, as he drags a dazed Demitri up off the floor and holds him upright with his arms behind his back.

"*Matteo!*" I hear Aria screaming from the corner of the room, and when I glance over my shoulder and see her with her knees braced up to her chest, panting, I know I have to make this quick

"You're lucky she needs me. I'd have liked to have made this much slower." I reach down for the knife that I always keep strapped to my ankle, and just as he goes to say something, I slice the blade across his throat. Blood flows from the gash like a river, and when Aria's father lets his body slump to the floor, I look down at my best friend and feel an unexpected pang of sadness.

"Go be with her." Stevan's voice shakes me out of the trance I'm in, as he looks across the room at his daughter. And I waste no more time, rushing over to my wife and dropping to my knees beside her.

"Is he dead?" she manages, in between the breaths she's making.

"He's dead," I assure her, taking her hand and letting her squeeze it.

Did you love her?" She forces her words out, as her face screws up with pain.

"Love who?"

"The woman you were having a child with. You told me you only ever....Holy fuck, this hurts!" Her hand shakes as her nails dig into my palm.

"No, I didn't love her. The child wasn't planned, but that doesn't mean I didn't grieve it," I tell her, swiping away the hair that's stuck to her forehead and fallen into her eyes. "But none of that matters, now. What matters, is this."

"He's coming, Matteo, it's too early and he's coming. What if something goes wrong?" She starts sobbing and I feel completely fucking helpless.

"Nothing's going to go wrong. He's gonna be fine, just concentrate and listen to what Anita tells you. She's delivered lots of babies, she knows what she's doing." Anita looks up at me and raises her brow because she knows, as well as I do, that I'm lying, and when I throw her a stern look of warning, she strokes the shaking leg that Aria has balanced over her shoulder.

"What if he's coming out the wrong way, or if he's too big?" Aria continues to freak out and I realize I have to put all my own fears aside and take some control of the situation.

"Listen to me." I grab her face in my hands and force her eyes onto mine.

"You are doing great, you are going to push as hard as you can and our son is going to be fine," I tell her firmly, and when she nods back at me, through her tears, I quickly release her and take hold of her hand, again.

"He's definitely not coming out the wrong way, I can see his head." Anita looks up at Aria with a reassuring smile on her face. Hearing that seems to give Aria a new strength, she presses the back of her head against the wall behind her, tensing her whole body as she pushes.

"I can't deliver my baby in the same room as a dead man," she tells me through her gritted teeth.

"I'm on it." Her father quickly grabs Demitri by his ankles and starts dragging him out the cabin, leaving a thick trail of blood in his path, while Aria continues to push.

"The head's out. He's almost here!" Anita's voice comes out excited.

"You hear that? It's almost over, you're gonna have our little boy in your arms any minute, Aria," I tell her, shrugging out my jacket and passing it to Anita so she'll have something to wrap him in.

"It hurts. I wanted drugs," she cries, taking a breath before the next contraction hits her.

"We'll get you drugs for the next one, I promise" I assure her, and when both her, and Anita, give me the same shocked look, I wonder which one of them is going to punch me first. I smile back at my wife, awkwardly, and she proves she isn't mad when she makes that cute, little laugh. It only lasts until her next contraction hits, and her face suddenly turns serious, again.

She growls like a tiger, pushing so hard that her skin turns red and her whole body shakes.

"Shoulders are out... and tummy... and legs and...he's here!" Anita yells, over the sound of crying. When I look down into her arms and see my son, wailing, and wiggling his limbs, I glance back to Aria and see overwhelment on her face, too.

"He's here." I can hardly believe my own words, as I stare at the tiny person we made, who is finally with us.

"And he's perfect." Anita wraps him up in my suit jacket and places him in his mother's arms, and Aria kisses his tiny, little head despite all the blood and shit that's stuck to it.

"You did it." I kiss her hard on her lips before looking at my son again. He's still screaming his lungs out, but it's the sweetest sound I ever heard, and when I wrap them both up in my arms, for the first time in my life I feel like I did something good.

CHAPTER THIRTY-NINE

ARIA

Anita managed to cut our baby's cord using the equipment Demitri had in his bag, and when Dr Fabier arrived shortly afterwards, he helped me deliver the placenta. Both my father and Matteo argued against me when I refused to go to hospital, which at least proves they have the ability to agree on something. But after getting a clean bill of health for both me and the baby from Dr Fabier, Matteo agreed with some persuasion that we could go straight home.

Now I'm home and lying in bed, holding our perfect, little boy, what happened a few hours ago at the cabin feels like a lifetime ago.

"I can't believe he was going to do that to you!" Matteo paces at the bottom of the bed. Seeing all the surgical equipment Demitri had, in preparation to take our child, has really freaked him out. I'm far too tired and overwhelmed with love to let those thoughts back in my head.

"We're okay, now," I assure him, patting the mattress beside me for him to come and join us.

"Look how perfect he is, he has your nose." I smile up at my husband, relieved to see that all his anger has vanished when he looks down at our son.

"Can I come in?" The door creaks open and when my father steps through it, Matteo doesn't tense the way I expect him to. In fact, he stands up from the bed and welcomes him.

"Would you like to hold your grandson?" he offers, shocking me when he lifts our newborn son out of my arms to place him in the crook of my father's.

I've never seen so much emotion on my father's face as he looks down and smiles proudly.

"You should get that shoulder seen to," he tells Matteo, clearing his throat when he finds himself getting a little choked.

"What shoulder?" I look between them in confusion.

"When the gun went off, I got caught," Matteo admits like it's no big deal.

"It would have been fatal if it wasn't for your father." He nods gratefully at him before taking our son out of his arms and bringing him back to me.

"I'm gonna say this in front of her because we no longer keep secrets from each other." Matteo sits beside me and takes my hand, as he addresses my father.

"I took your daughter with the wrong intention, I did it to make you hurt, because I thought you were to blame for what I lost. The only intention I have now, is to love her, keep her safe and make her happy. Are you going to try and stand in my way?" Matteo asks him outright, keeping his face stern and his eyes focused.

"Is this what you want?" My father looks at me, thoughtfully.

"When did it ever matter to you what I wanted?" I answer him back, thinking about Dennis and all the men he lined me up, to marry, before him.

"Aria, there's something you should know about me. All my

life I've perceived myself to be a man who should be feared. But all I really am is a man who plays with other people's money. For a long time, I got lucky with the deals I made. People who invested in me always got their payout, but I knew it wouldn't last forever. Those marriages I arranged were unfair, but they were always for your protection. I loved your mother very much. She was taken from me in the worst possible way, and all my life I have feared you meeting a man, like this one." His eyes shift toward Matteo. "A man like me, whose love would make you a target."

"I was told my mother was a whore." I shake my head at him.

"Aria, your mother was my everything." Matteo moves, so my father can perch next to me on the bed and take my hand.

"Angelo Romano had her taken, and tortured, just after you were born, I used his money for a deal, and it went very wrong. I couldn't pay him back. Your mother paid the price for that." I look at Matteo and realize he looks every bit as shocked as I am.

"I always feared that he, or someone else, would have taken you too, so I made out to everyone, even those close to me, that you were a burden. I arranged for you to marry men who could financially support you but not make you a target."

"Aria, I had no idea." Matteo shakes his head, and I feel the tears roll out of my eyes when it sinks in what really happened to my mom.

"I haven't behaved like a father, I understand that now. But the fear I felt when you were gone…I don't want to lose you. I've misled you, and many others in the past, but I want to make it right. Does this man make you happy, Aria?" He smiles at me through tear-filled eyes.

"Very," I assure him.

"Then, no, I won't stand in your way, Matteo Romano." He

looks up to Matteo and holds out his hand, a hand that Matteo takes and shakes firmly.

"The past is in the past. Like I told you before, I would never have blamed a son for the sins of his father, any feud we had is over," my father confirms, and when my son starts to squawk and his mouth seeks me out, I look at him and smile awkwardly.

"I'll leave you to that. I will visit again in a few days if that's okay?" He looks to Matteo as he stands back up.

"You will always be welcome." Matteo nods, and after seeing him to the door, he joins me back on the bed to watch our son feed from me.

"You're fucking incredible, you know that?" he tells me, stroking our little boy's cheek.

"Have you ever seen anything more beautiful?" I look down at him and my eyes brim with tears of pride. Matteo surprises me when he grabs my chin and forces my head to twist and look at him.

"I won't ever regret taking you. You taught me how to feel something other than hate and I've learned that I can love." He kisses me hard on the lips before releasing me, then strokes our son's head as he continues to feed. I rest my head on my husband's shoulder and take everything in. Leaving all the bad behind us and focusing on what's good. Our child may have been created out of vengeance, but he will be raised among love.

EPILOGUE

MATTEO

"Mrs Romano, you should let me do that," Anita argues with my wife, and when she notices me creeping into the room carrying our son, she shrugs at me, helplessly.

"Yes, Mrs Romano, you should." My wife turns around when she hears my voice and immediately looks guilty.

"I was just..." She bites her lip like she thinks it'll get her out of trouble, and I slowly move towards her, rolling my eyes and offering my hand to help her down from the chair she's standing on. "...I want everything to be perfect. You know how critical your mom can be." She looks around the room at the hundreds of balloons that are pinned to the ceiling.

"You better not have done all this by yourself." I look around the over-decorated room, as I splay my palm over her huge stomach. Our son has only just reached his first birthday, and Aria is already close to giving birth to our second child.

"Tomas did most of it," she assures me, taking our son from my arms and rubbing her nose against his before she balances him on her hip.

I can't help admiring the view, Aria is a fantastic mother,

and seeing her holding our son, while her belly swells with our daughter, makes me wonder how the hell I got so lucky.

"What time is your father getting here?" I tug them both close and kiss her, her lips taste like strawberries and I get the sudden urge to be inside her, again. Pregnancy makes Aria insatiable, and it's been at least six hours since I last made her come.

The doorbell rings right on cue and Aria smiles at me as she places Oliver back into my arms.

"That will be him right now." She plants another kiss on me before waddling off to answer it.

I spend the next few hours making polite conversation with Aria's father and ensuring Mom's glass stays topped up. Aria wanted to make Oliver's first birthday special, and like everything she does, she's done the perfect job. She has the biggest smile on her face as she watches her father play on the floor with Oliver, and when Mom comments on how delicious the cake, she spent hours baking is, Aria almost knocks the Martini out of her hand when she hugs her.

As the afternoon goes on, I notice Aria starting to look tired, and when everybody leaves, I force her to go upstairs for a nap. I spend some time playing with Oliver. Watching him grow feels like the greatest gift in the world, and if I thought falling for Aria had changed my life, having him come into it completely spun it on its axis. I want to take away all the bad from the world for him, and as I lie beside him on the floor, watching him push the train that Stevan gifted him along the rug, I wonder if the empire that my family has built will be a burden to him.

I've made a lot of changes since he was born and secured some investments that will ensure he has a choice over what kind of man he will become.

When I notice him starting to tire too, I carry him up the

stairs and bathe him then, putting him in his crib, I watch him till he falls asleep. Aria refuses to have a nanny, she wants to witness every precious moment for herself. Usually bath and bedtime is something we all do together, but being pregnant while chasing around after a one-year-old is starting to take its toll on her.

When Oliver is fast asleep, I place a kiss on his forehead and head out onto the landing. I nod at the guard, who stands outside his room, before moving down the hall to check on my wife.

I'm surprised when I find our bed empty, and after checking the bathroom and still not locating her, I figure she must be in the kitchen. This time around Aria has become addicted to sweet things, pickles actually make her throw up, and she can't get enough of cookie dough. I'm already thinking of ways we can get inventive with that when I feel my phone vibrate in my pocket.

Taking it out, I check the screen and feel the dark smile lift on my lips as I read what it says.

    Meet me in the basement.

I find my wife standing against the back wall, wearing the black, lace underwear I used, to limit her to. Her huge bump is on full display and she has the collar, that's still attached to the wall, fastened around her neck. My cock instantly goes hard, and I slowly slide my finger across my bottom lip as I start walking towards her.

"What is this?" I ask, trying my best to hide my smirk.

"This is us." She shrugs her shoulders and smiles, "It's how we first started, and tonight it's how I want to be fucked." Hearing her curse makes my palms twitchy, and I lick my lips, while I decide if I'm going to be a victim of her temptation or not.

Aria knows that I take her delicate condition very seriously, but I'm not a man whose limits should be tested. It appears that my beautiful wife has much more faith in me than I do.

She patiently waits for my response and I see the shock and thrill sparkle in her eyes when I grip my hand around her dainty little throat and pin her against the wall.

"Speak your name," I command, the same way I did the first time I saw her down here.

"You know my fucking name." She smiles, as she plays along.

"I didn't ask you to tell me it. I *asked* you to speak it." I narrow my eyes at her.

"Aria Romano." She speaks her name, slowly and seductively, and I reward her by sliding my hand over the swell of her stomach and slipping it into her panties.

"You are very wet, Aria Romano." I tease her with my finger, listening to her breaths becoming heavier. "You want to be fucked tonight, wearing this collar?" I grip it with my hand as I push two of my fingers inside her and watch the swallow, she makes, travel down her throat.

"Yes," she manages, closing her eyes and bucking herself against my hand. "You look stunning when you're desperate," I tell her, sliding my free hand down her body and resting it on the ridge of her bump. I wait until she's come all over my fingers before I spin her body around, taking both her hands in mine and bracing them against the wall in front of her.

"Spread your legs for me," I demand, gathering her long hair in my hand and holding it in a ponytail. "You know, from the back, you can't even tell you're pregnant." I massage her shoulder with my other hand, and she rears her little ass up against me, trying so hard to get the friction she needs.

"Look at you, ready to give birth any day and still craving my cock." I make sure she hears my belt buckle clink as I undo it, and when I unzip my slacks and take it out, I stroke it through my palm, making sure the tip only just touches the base of her spine.

"Matteo, please," she begs, and when she slides one of her hands down from the wall, so she can try and relieve some of the tension between her legs, I land my palm on her ass cheek just hard enough to make her squeal.

"I can't wait to be able to mark you, again," I tell her, soothing my hand over the cheek I just spanked before gripping it tightly.

"Please. I..." The words get trapped in her mouth when I bend my knees and agonizingly, slowly fill her with my cock. I love the long, satisfied sigh of relief she makes when she has every single inch of it and I hold still inside her.

"I'm going to fuck you fast, I'm going to fuck you hard. And I'm going to fuck you, like the girl I brought here to ruin," I warn, cradling her huge stomach in my hands as I do exactly what I promised. Aria knows that she can be as loud as she wants to be down here, and she takes full advantage of that. Screaming my name and moaning loudly as she comes, again and again, dripping all over my thick, hard cock. She scratches at the walls, her legs tremble, and when I feel my own release coming I sink my teeth into her shoulder and fill her warm, tight cunt with my cum. My head spins as I hold her steady, and just when I start to worry that I've been too rough, she stretches her arms up so she can wrap them behind my neck, forcing her tight, swollen stomach to stick out even more.

"That was just what I needed," she sighs, snuggling her

head into the crook of my neck. "What shall we do with the rest of our night?"

"I was planning on taking you upstairs, drawing you a bath and taking care of you." I make a long, circular stroke around her belly, pausing when I feel our little girl push out against my palm.

"Whatever happened to you, Matteo Romano?" Aria laughs, and I quickly spin her back around to face me, hooking my hand into the collar she's wearing, and using it to draw her to my lips.

"I found the girl who ruined me." I force my tongue into her mouth and kiss her the way she likes to be kissed. Rough, firm and like she belongs to me.

THE END

ABOUT THE AUTHOR

Come stalk/find me here.

facebook.com/authorlilahraine
instagram.com/authorlilahraine

Printed in Great Britain
by Amazon